The Human Vampire

Someone knocks at the door of the Las Vegas home where I stand. It is late evening; the living room is dimly lit, four walls of blurred shadows. I don't know who this person is. For that matter, I'm not sure who I am. I have just awakened from a dead alchemist's experiment. My mind is foggy and my nerves are shot. But before I embarked on the experiment, only hours ago, I was a steel-willed vampire—the last vampire on earth. Now I fear—and hope—that I may once again be human. That I may be a young woman named Alisa, the humble offspring of a five-thousand-year-old monster called Sita.

The person continues to knock.

"Open the door," he says impatiently. "It's me."

Who is me? I wonder.

Books by Christopher Pike

BURY ME DEEP
CHAIN LETTER 2: THE ANCIENT EVIL
DIE SOFTLY
THE ETERNAL ENEMY
FALL INTO DARKNESS
FINAL FRIENDS #1: THE PARTY
FINAL FRIENDS #2: THE DANCE
FINAL FRIENDS #3: THE GRADUATION
GIMME A KISS
THE IMMORTAL
LAST ACT
THE LAST VAMPIRE
THE LAST VAMPIRE 2: BLACK BLOOD
THE LAST VAMPIRE 3: RED DICE
THE LAST VAMPIRE 4: PHANTOM
THE LOST MIND
MASTER OF MURDER
THE MIDNIGHT CLUB
MONSTER
REMEMBER ME
REMEMBER ME 2: THE RETURN
REMEMBER ME 3: THE LAST STORY
ROAD TO NOWHERE
SCAVENGER HUNT
SEE YOU LATER
SPELLBOUND
THE STARLIGHT CRYSTAL
THE VISITOR
WHISPER OF DEATH
THE WICKED HEART
WITCH

Available from ARCHWAY Paperbacks

Christopher Pike

The Last Vampire 4

PHANTOM

AN ARCHWAY PAPERBACK
Published by POCKET BOOKS
New York London Toronto Sydney Tokyo Singapore

This book is a work of fiction. Names, characters, places and incidents are products of the author's imagination or are used fictitiously. Any resemblance to actual events or locales or persons, living or dead, is entirely coincidental.

AN ARCHWAY PAPERBACK *Original*

 An Archway Paperback published by
POCKET BOOKS, a division of Simon & Schuster Inc.
1230 Avenue of the Americas, New York, NY 10020

Copyright © 1996 by Christopher Pike

ISBN: 0-671-55030-6

First Archway Paperback printing May 1996

10 9 8 7 6 5 4 3 2 1

AN ARCHWAY PAPERBACK and colophon are registered trademarks of Simon & Schuster Inc.

Cover art by Jeff Walker

Printed in the U.S.A.

IL 9+

For Scott, who loves female vampires

The Last Vampire 4

PHANTOM

1

Someone knocks at the door of the Las Vegas home where I stand. It is late evening; the living room is dimly lit, four walls of blurred shadows. I don't know who this person is. For that matter, I'm not sure who I am. I have just awakened from a dead alchemist's experiment. My mind is foggy and my nerves are shot. But before I embarked on the experiment, only hours ago, I was a steel-willed vampire—the last vampire on earth. Now I fear—and hope—that I may once again be human. That I may be a young woman named Alisa, the humble offspring of a five-thousand-year-old monster called Sita.

The person continues to knock.

"Open the door," he says impatiently. "It's me."

Who is me? I wonder. I do not recognize the voice,

1

although it does sound familiar. Yet I hesitate to obey, even to respond. Of those few I call friends, only Seymour Dorsten is supposed to know I am in this Las Vegas home. My other friends—well, a couple recently perished in the Nevada desert, in a nuclear blast. A lot has been happening in the last few days, and most of it has been my doing.

"Sita," the person outside the door says. "I know you're in there."

Curious, I think. He knows my ancient name. He even says it like he knows me. But why doesn't he tell me his name? I could ask him, but some emotion stops me. It is one I have seldom known in my five thousand years.

Fear. I stare down at my hands.

I tremble with fear. If I am human, I know, I am practically defenseless. That is why I do not want to open the door. I do not want to die before I have had a chance to taste mortality. Before I have had the opportunity to have a child. That is perhaps the primary reason I employed Arturo's alchemetic tools to reverse my vampirism—to become a mother. Yet I am still not a hundred percent sure the experiment has succeeded. I reach down with the nails of my right hand and pinch my left palm. The flesh breaks; there is a line of blood. I stare at it.

The wound does not immediately heal.

I must be human. Lord Krishna save me.

The knocking stops. The person outside takes a step back from the door. I hear his movements, even with my mediocre human ears. He seems to chuckle to himself.

"I understand, Sita," he says. "It's all right. I'll return soon."

I hear him walk away. Only then do I realize I have been standing in the dark with my breath held. Almost collapsing from relief, I sag against the door and try to calm my thumping heart. I am both confused and exalted.

"I am human," I whisper to myself.

Tears roll over my face. I touch them with my quivering tongue. They are clear and salty, not dark and bloody. Another sign that I am human. Moving slowly, striving to maintain my balance, I step to the living room couch and sit down. Looking around, I marvel at how blurred everything is, and wonder if the experiment has damaged my eyesight. But then I realize I must be seeing things as a human sees, which means to see so little. Why, I can't even distinguish the grain in the wood panel on the far wall. Nor can I hear the voices of the people in the cars that pass outside. I am virtually blind and deaf.

"I am human," I repeat in wonder. Then I begin to laugh, to cry some more, and to wonder what the hell I'm going to do next. Always, as a vampire, I could do anything I wished. Now I doubt if I will ever leave the house.

I pick up the remote and turn on the TV. The news—they are talking about the hydrogen bomb that exploded in the desert the previous night. They say it destroyed a top-secret military base. The wind was blowing away from Las Vegas so the fallout should be almost nonexistent. They don't say anything about me, however, even though I was there and witnessed the whole thing. The experts wonder if it was an accident. They don't connect it to the mass police killings I committed in Los Angeles a few days earlier. They are not very imaginative, I think. They don't believe in vampires.

And now there are no more vampires to believe in.

"I beat you, Yaksha," I say aloud to my dead creator, the vampire who sucked my blood five thousand years ago and replaced it with his own mysterious fluids. "It took me a long time but now I can go back to an ordinary life."

Yet my memories are not ordinary. My mind is not either, although I suddenly realize I am having trouble remembering many things that hours ago were clear. Has my identity changed with my body? What percentage of personal ego is constructed from memory? True, I still remember Krishna, but I can no longer see him in my mind's eye as I could before. I forget even the blue of his eyes—that unfathomable blue, as dear as the most polished star in the black heavens. The realization saddens me. My long life has been littered with pain, but also much joy. I do not want it to be forgotten, especially by me.

"Joel," I whisper. "Arturo."

I will not forget them. Joel was an FBI agent, a friend I made into a vampire in order to save his life. An alteration that caused him to die from a nuclear bomb. And Arturo, another friend, a hybrid of humanity and vampires from the Middle Ages, my personal priest, my passionate lover, and the greatest alchemist in history. It was Arturo who forced me to detonate the bomb, and destroy him and Joel, but my love for him is still warm and near. I only wish he were with me now to see what miracle his esoteric knowledge has wrought. But would the vampire blood–obsessed Arturo have still loved my human body? Yes, dear Arturo, I believe so. I still believe in you.

Then there was Ray, my Rama reincarnated. My memories of him will never fade, I swear, even if my human brain eventually grows forgetful. My love for Ray is not a human or vampire creation. It is beyond understanding, eternal, even though he himself is dead. Killed trying to kill a demon, the malignant Eddie Fender. There are worse reasons to die, I suppose. I still remember more than a few of them.

Yet, at the moment, I do not want to dwell on the past.

I just want to be human again. And live.

There comes another knock at the front door.

I become very still. How quickly frightened a human can become.

"Sita," this person calls. "It's me, Seymour. Can I come in?"

This voice I definitely recognize. Standing with effort, I walk to the front door and undo the lock and chain. Seymour stands on the porch and stares at me. He wears the same thick glasses and hopelessly mismatched clothes of the high school nerd I met in a stupid PE class only a few months before. His face changes as he studies me; his expression turns to one of alarm. He has trouble speaking.

"It worked," he gasps.

I smile and open the door all the way. "It worked. Now I am like you. Now I am free of the curse."

Seymour shakes his head as he steps in the house and I close the door. He liked me as a vampire, I know. He wanted me to make him a vampire, to poison him through the metamorphosis, an act that was strictly forbidden by Krishna five thousand years ago. Now Seymour is upset. Unable to sit, he paces in front of me. There are unshed tears in his eyes.

"Why did you do it?" he demands. "I didn't think you would really do it."

I force my smile wider and spread my arms. "But you knew I would. And I want you to be happy for me." I gesture for him to come to me. "Give me a hug, and this time I won't be able to squeeze you to death."

He hugs me, reluctantly, and as he does so he finally does shed his tears. He has to turn away; he is having trouble breathing. Naturally his reaction upsets me.

"It's gone," he says to the far wall.

"What's gone?"

"The magic is gone."

I speak firmly. "It is only Yaksha's blood that has been destroyed. Maybe you don't like that. Maybe your fantasies of being a vampire are ruined. But think of the world—it is safe now from this curse. And only you and I know how close it came to being destroyed by it."

But Seymour shakes his head as he glances at me. "I am not worried about my own personal fantasies. Yeah, sure, I wanted to be a vampire. What eighteen-year-old wouldn't want to be one? But the magic is gone. You were that magic."

My cheek twitches; his words wound me. "I am still here. I am still Alisa."

"But you are no longer Sita. The world needed her in order to be a place of mystery. Even before I met you, I *knew* you. You know I knew you. I wrote my stories late at night and your darkness filled them." He hung his head. "Now the world is empty. It's nothing."

I approach and touch his arm. "My feelings for you have not changed. Are they nothing? Good God, Seymour, you speak to me as if I were dead."

He touches my hand but now it is hard for him to look at me. "Now you will die."

"All who are born die," I say, quoting Krishna. "All who are dead will be reborn. It is the nature of things."

He bites his lower lip and stares at the floor. "That's easy to say but it's not easy to live through. When you met me, I had AIDS. My death was certain—it was all I could see. It was like a slow-motion horror film that never ended. It was only your blood that saved me." He pauses. "How many others could it have saved?"

"Now you sound like Arturo."

"He was a brilliant man."

"He was a dangerous man."

Seymour shrugs. "You alwa~~ everything. I can't talk ~~

"But you can. ~~

listen as well. You have to give me a chance to explain how I feel. I'm happy the experiment has succeeded. It means more to me than you can imagine. And I'm happy there's no going back."

He catches my eye. "Is that true?"

"You know it is true. There is no more vampire blood, anywhere. It's over." I squeeze his arm and pull him closer. "Let it be over. I need you now, you know, more than I needed you before." I bury my face in his shoulder. "You have to teach me how to be a nerd."

My small joke makes him chuckle. "Can we have sex now?" he asks.

I raise my head and plant a wet kiss on his cheek. "Sure. When we're both a little older." I shake him, but not so hard as I used to. "How dare you ask me a question like that? We haven't been on a date yet."

He tries hard to accept the loss of his world, the death of his magic. He forces a smile. "There's a vampire movie in town. We could see it, and eat popcorn, and jeer, and then have sex afterward." He waits for an answer. "It's what most nerd couples do every Saturday evening."

I suddenly remember. It has taken me this long. There must be something wrong with my mind. I turn away and swear under my breath. "Damn."

"What is it?" he asks. "You don't like popcorn?"

"We have to get out of town. We have to leave now."

"Why?"

"There was someone here a few minutes ago. A
___man—he was knocking at the door."

"Who was it?"

"I don't know. I didn't open the door. But this guy—he called me by name. He called me Sita. He kept insisting I open the door."

"Why didn't you?"

"Because I didn't know who he was! Because I'm human now!" I pause and frown. "His voice sounded familiar. I swear, I knew it, but I just can't place it."

"What makes you think he's dangerous?"

"Do you have to ask that question? No one alive, except you, knows me by the name Sita." I stop again. "He said he would come back. He laughed as he said it. He sounded so sure of himself."

"What else did he say?"

"He called himself my darling."

Seymour was thoughtful. "Could Arturo have survived the blast?"

"No."

"But he was a hybrid. Half human, half vampire. It's possible. Don't dismiss the possibility."

I shake my head. "Even Yaksha could not have survived that blast."

"But you did."

"I floated away at the last minute. You know, I told you." I turn toward the kitchen, my car keys. "The sooner we leave the better."

Seymour grabs my arm. "I disagree. You have said there are no more vampires. What do we have to fear from this person? Better we stay and find out who he is."

I consider. "The government must have known Arturo was using this house. Such records were bly kept somewhere else besides the army base I destroyed. The government might be watching this house now."

"But you said you knew this person."

"I'm not sure about that. There was something in his voice, though . . ."

"What?" Seymour demands when I don't finish.

I strain to remember through my newfound human fog. "His tone—it gave me a chill."

Seymour acts like a wise guy. "In the real world not everybody who comes to the front door wants to kill you. Some guys just want to sell you a vacuum cleaner."

I remain stubborn. "We're getting out of here now." Grabbing the keys off the kitchen table, I peer out the back window and see nothing significant. In the distance, the lights of the Strip come alive and shimmer, colored beacons in a desert wasteland. A nuclear bomb just exploded but human vice will not be postponed. Of course the wind was blowing the other way, but I do not judge. I have always been a gambler. I understand better than most why the atomic dice did not betray the city of sin. Why the fallout fell the other way. Still, I swear again. "Damn. I wish I had my old vision right now. Just for a minute."

"And I bet your old hearing." Seymour comes up at my side and pats me on the back. "You're going to make that same wish a lot of times in the next few days."

2 ~~~

I own houses all over the world, some modest places to relax when I enter a foreign country in search of fresh blood, others so extravagant one would think I was an Arabian princess. My home in Beverly Hills, where we drive after leaving Las Vegas, is one of the most opulent ones. As we enter the front door, Seymour stares in wonder.

"If we stay here," he says, "I have to get new clothes."

"You can have the clothes, but we're not staying. Ray's father knew about this house, so the government might as well. We're just here to get money, credit cards, clothes, and fresh identification."

Seymour is doubtful. "The government knew you

were at the compound. They'll think you died in the blast."

"They'll have to know for sure that I died. They were obsessed with my blood, so they'll research every possible lead concerning me." I step to the window and peer outside. It is the middle of the night. "They may be watching us now."

Seymour shrugs. "Are you going to get me fresh ID?"

I glance at him. "You should go home."

He shakes his head firmly. "I'm not going to leave you. Forget it. I mean, you don't even know how to be human."

I step past him. "We can discuss this later. We don't want to be here a minute more than we have to be."

In the basement of my Beverly Hills home, I pick up the things I mentioned to Seymour. I also take a 9mm Smith & Wesson equipped with a silencer and several rounds of ammunition. My reflexes and vision are not what they used to be, but I believe I am still an excellent shot. All my supplies I load into a large black leather suitcase. I am surprised how much it weighs as I carry it back upstairs. My physical weakness is disconcerting.

I don't let Seymour see the gun.

We leave Beverly Hills and drive toward Santa Monica. I let Seymour drive; the speed of the surrounding cars disturbs me. It is as if I am a young woman from 3000 B.C. who has been plucked from her slow-paced world and dumped into the dizzyingly fast twentieth century. I tell myself I just need time to get used to it. My euphoria over being human remains, but the anxiety is there as well.

Who was at the door?

I can't imagine. Not even a single possibility comes to mind. But there was something about that voice.

We check into a Sheraton hotel by the beach. My new name is Candice Hall. Seymour is just a friend helping me with my bags. I don't put his name down on the register. I will not stay Candice long. I have other ID that I can change my hair style and color to match, as well as other small features. Yet I feel safe as I close the door of the hotel room behind me. Since Las Vegas, I have kept an eye on the rearview mirror. I don't believe we've been followed. Seymour sets my bag on the floor as I plop down on the bed and sigh.

"I haven't felt this exhausted in a long time," I say.

Seymour sits beside me. "We humans are always tired."

"I am going to enjoy being human. I don't care what you say."

He stares at me in the dimly lit room. "Sita?"

I close my eyes and yawn. "Yes?"

"I am sorry what I said. If this makes you happy, then it makes me happy."

"Thank you."

"I just worry, you know, that there's no going back."

I sit up and touch his leg. "The decision would have been meaningless if I could have gone back."

He understands my subtle meaning. "You didn't do this because of what Krishna said to you about vampires?" he asks.

I nod. "I think partly. I don't think Krishna approved of vampires. I think he just allowed me to live out of his deep compassion for all living things."

"Maybe there was another reason."

"Perhaps." I touch his face. "Did I ever tell you how dear you are to me?"

He smiles. "No. You were always too busy threatening to kill me."

I feel a stab of pain. It is in my chest, where a short time ago a stake pierced my heart. For a moment the area is raw with an agonizing burning, as if I am bleeding to death. But it is a brief spasm. I draw in a shuddering breath and speak in a sad voice.

"I always kill the ones I love."

He takes my hand. "That was before. It can be different now that you're not a monster."

I have to laugh, although it is still not easy to take a deep breath. "Is that a line you use to get a girl to go to bed with you?"

He leans closer. "I already have you in bed."

I roll onto my side. "I need to take a shower. We both need to rest."

He draws back, disappointed. "You haven't changed that much."

I stand and fluff up his hair, trying to cheer him up. "But I have. I'm a nineteen-year-old girl again. You just forget what monsters teenage girls can be."

He is suddenly moved. "I never knew the exact age you were when Yaksha changed you."

I pause and think of Rama, my long dead husband, and Lalita, my daughter, cremated fifty centuries ago in a place I was never to know.

"Yes," I say softly. "I was almost twenty when Yaksha came for me." And because I was suspended so long between the ages, I add again, "Almost."

An hour later Seymour is fast asleep beside me on the king-size bed. But despite my physical exhaustion, my mind refuses to shut down. I can't be free of the images of Joel's and Arturo's faces from two nights earlier when I suddenly began to turn to light, to dissolve, to leave them just before the bomb was detonated. At the time I knew I was dead. It was a certainty. Yet one last miracle occurred and I lived on. Perhaps there was a reason.

I climb out of bed and dress. Before leaving the hotel room, I load my pistol and tuck it in my belt, at the back, pulling my sweatshirt over it.

The hotel is located on Ocean Ave. I cross over it, and the Coast Highway that separates me from the ocean. Soon I am walking along the dark and foggy Santa Monica Beach, not the safest place to be in the early morning hours before the sun rises. Yet I walk briskly, heading south, paying little attention to my surroundings. What work it is to make my legs move over the sand! It is as if I walk with weights strapped around my ankles. Sweat drips in my eyes and I pant audibly. But I feel good as well. Finally, after thirty minutes of toil, my mind begins to relax, and I contemplate returning to the hotel and trying to sleep. It is only then that I become aware that two men are following me.

They are fifty yards behind me. In the dark it is hard to distinguish their features, but it is clear they are both Caucasian and well built, maybe thirty years old. They move like two good ol' boys, one dark featured, ugly, the other bright as a bottle of beer foaming in the sunlight. I think these boys have been drinking beer—and stronger—and are feeling uncomfortably horny. I smile to myself as I anticipate the encounter, even imagine what their blood will taste like. Then I remember I am not who I used to be. A wave of fear sweeps through my body, but I stand and wait for them to come to me.

"Hey, girl," the one with dark hair says with a Southern accent. "What are you doing out at this time of night?"

I shrug. "Just out for a walk. What are you guys up to?"

The blond guy snickers. "How old are you, girl?"

"Why?" I ask.

The dark-haired one moves slightly to my left. He flexes his fists as he speaks. "We just want to know if you're legal."

"I'm old enough to vote," I say. "Not old enough to drink. You boys been drinking tonight?"

They both chuckle. The blond guy moves a step closer. He smells of beer, whiskey. "You might say we've been looking at the wrong end of a few bottles tonight. But don't let that worry you none. We're still fully capable of finishing what we start."

I take a step back. Perhaps it's a mistake that I show fear. "I don't want any trouble," I say. And I mean it, although I feel as if I can still take them. After all, I am still a master of martial arts. A series of swift kicks to their groins, their jaws, should settle any unpleasantness. The dark-haired guy steps off to my left, and wipes at his slobbering mouth with the back of his arm.

"We don't want trouble either," he says. "We're just looking for a good time."

I catch his eye, and really do wish that my stare was still capable of burning into his brain. Seymour was right—my wishes have already settled into a pattern of wanting what I have lost. Yet I do my best to make my voice hard.

"Sometimes a good time can cost you," I say.

"I don't think so," the blond guy says. "You agree, John?"

"She looks like a freebie to me, Ed," John responds.

They've used their names in front of me. That is a bad sign. It means they're either too drunk to know better, or else they plan to kill me. The latter seems a distinct possibility since they clearly intend to rape me. I take another step back, and am tempted to reach for my gun. Yet I don't really want to kill them, especially since there is no need for their blood. Knocking them unconscious is my preference.

Actually, it is my second preference. Surviving is my first.

"If you touch me I'll scream," I warn them.

"No one's going to hear you down here," John says as he reaches out to grab me. "Take her, Ed!"

They go for me simultaneously, John close on my left, Ed three feet in front of me. But it is John who reaches me first. He has pretty good reflexes for a drunk. Before I can twist away, he catches me in a bear hug. Briefly I struggle, and then go limp. When

Ed closes within two feet, however, I shove back against John and jump up, lifting both my feet off the ground. Lashing out with the right, I catch Ed in the groin. He shouts in pain and doubles up.

"The bitch got me!" he complains.

"Goddamn it!" John yells in my ear. "You're going to pay for that."

In response I slash backward and up with my left elbow. The blow catches John square on the jaw and his hold on me loosens as he staggers back. In an instant I am free. Since Ed is still bent over, I do him the favor of kicking him in the face, breaking his nose. He drops to his knees, his face dark with blood.

"Help me, John," he moans.

"Help him, John," I mock as John regains his balance and glares at me with death in his eyes. I gesture with my little finger. "Come on, John. Come and get your good-time girl."

John charges like a bull. I leap up and lash out with my left foot in order to kiss his jaw with the heel of my boot. The only trouble is that my timing and balance are all off. I have not risen far enough off the ground. Instead of striking him in the face, I hit him just above the heart, and the blow has not nearly the power I anticipated. John is a big man, over two hundred pounds. He grunts in pain as I strike but he doesn't stop. The momentum of his charge brushes aside my leg and now it is me who is suddenly off balance.

Frantically, I try to bring my left leg back in beneath me before I land but I am too late. With a thud, I topple on my right foot and hit the sand with the right side of my face. John is on me in a second, grabbing me from behind and pinning my arms midway up my spine. He's strong. My upper vertebrae feel as if they will explode. With his free hand he smacks me on the back of the head.

"You are one nasty bitch," he swears as he presses my face into the sand. Straining, I twist my head to the side so that I can breathe and see what is going to happen to me. "Ed, give me a hand with this whore. She looked like a good sport to begin with but I'm afraid when we're done pleasing ourselves we're going to have to bury her in this spot."

"We'll let the crabs eat her," Ed agrees as he staggers over, still bleeding profusely from his smashed nose. Behind me, John reaches around for the button on my pants. That is something of a break because if he had just tried to pull my pants down from behind, he would have found the gun. Also, reaching around as he is, I realize, John is slightly off balance.

Digging in with my right knee and pushing off with the tip of my left foot, I shove up as hard as possible. The move catches John by surprise, and I momentarily break free and roll in the sand. But my freedom will be measured in fractions of a second if I don't take drastic action. Squirming onto my back, I see both John and Ed staring down at me with stupid grins. They look ten feet tall and as ugly as highway billboards. Together they reach for me.

"Wait!" I cry as I move my right hand slowly under my lower back. "If I lie still and cooperate will you please not hurt me?"

They pause to think about that. "You better lie still, bitch," John says finally. "But you've messed up my friend too much to just walk away from tonight."

"But we might give you a chance to crawl away," Ed says wiping at his bloody face and picking at his broken nose all in the same move.

"I won't leave here crawling," I say in a different tone of voice as my hand finds the butt of the gun. Leaning slightly to the left I whip it out and point it at the good ol' boys. They stare at it, frankly, as if they have never seen a gun before. Then they both take a step back. Maintaining my aim, I take my time getting back to my feet. I speak gently. "That's right boys," I say. "No sudden moves. No screams for help."

John chuckles uneasily. "Hey, you got us, girl. You got us good. We give you that. But you know we didn't mean you no harm. We just drank a little too much and didn't know what we were doing."

"We weren't going to hurt you none," Ed adds, sounding scared, as well he should. Still taking my time, I step within a foot of Ed and place the barrel of the gun between his eyebrows. His eyes get real big, and he wants to turn and run but I stop him with a faint shake of my head. To my left, John stands frozen in wonder and horror.

"You are both liars," I say in a cold voice. "You were not only going to rape me, you were going to kill me. Now I am going to kill you because you deserve to die. But you should be grateful I'm using a gun. A few nights ago I would have used my teeth and nails, and you would have died much slower." I pause. "Say goodbye to John, Ed."

Ed is consumed with murderer's remorse. "Please!" he says, his voice cracking. "I have a wife and kid back home. If I die, who will take care of them?"

"I've got two kids back home," John says passionately.

But I am unmoved. Being human has not made me more gullible.

Yet, I usually do not kill when I have the upper hand. I do not kill for pleasure. But I know these two will harm others in the future, and therefore it is better that they die now.

"It is better for your children not to grow up having to imitate trash like you," I say.

Ed's face is awash with tears. "No!" he cries.

"Yes," I say, and shoot him in the head. He falls hard.

I turn the gun on John, who slowly backs away, shaking his head.

"Have mercy," he pleads. "I don't want to die."

"Then you should never have been born," I reply.

I shoot him twice in the face. In the eyes.

Yet that is all I do. The ancient thirst is gone.

I leave their bodies for the crabs.

3 ~~~

It is only on the way back that the shock of what has just happened overwhelms me. Ordinarily, killing a couple of jerks would occupy my mind for less than ten seconds. But now it is as if I feel the trauma in every cell. My reaction is entirely human. As I stumble off the beach and back onto Ocean Ave., I shake visibly. I scarcely notice that I'm still carrying the gun in my right hand. Chiding myself, I hide it under my sweatshirt. If I was in my right mind I would throw it in the ocean in case I'm stopped and searched. But I'm reluctant to part with the gun. I feel so vulnerable; it is like a safety blanket to me.

There is a coffee shop open three blocks from the sea. Staggering inside, I take a booth in the corner and order a cup of black coffee. It is only when the steaming beverage arrives, and I wrap my trembling hands around the mug, that I notice the faint mist of blood splattered on the front of my gray sweatshirt. It must be on my face as well, and I reach up and brush at my skin, coming away with red-stained palms. What a fool I am, I think, to be out like this in public. I am on the verge of leaving when someone walks in the coffee shop, heads straight to my table, and sits down across from me.

It is Ray Riley. The love of my life.

He is supposed to be dead.

He nods slightly as he settles across from me, and I am struck by the fact that he is dressed exactly as when he ignited the gasoline truck outside the warehouse filled with Eddie Fender's evil vampires and blew himself to pieces. When he sacrificed his life to save mine. He wears a pair of black pants, a short-sleeved white silk shirt, Nike running shoes. His brown eyes are warm as always, his handsome face serious even though he wears a gentle smile. Yes, it is Ray. It is a miracle, and the sight of him stirs so much emotion inside me that I feel almost nothing. I am in shock, pure and simple. I can only stare with damp eyes and wonder if I am losing my mind.

"I know this is a surprise for you," he says softly.

I nod. Yes. A surprise.

"I know you thought I was dead," he continues. "And I think I was dead, for a time. When the truck exploded, I saw a bright flash of light. Then everything went black and I felt as if I were floating in the sky. But I couldn't see anything, know anything, even though I was not in pain. I don't know how long this continued. Eventually I became aware of my body again, but it was as if I was at a great distance from it. The strange thing was, I could feel only parts of it: a portion of my head, one throbbing hand, a burning sensation in my stomach. That was all at first. But slowly, more parts woke up, and I finally began to realize someone was trying to revive me by feeding me blood." He pauses. "Do you understand?"

I nod again. I am a statue. "Eddie," I whisper.

A spasm of pain crosses Ray's face. "Yes. Eddie collected what was left of me, and took me away to some dark cold place. There he fed me his blood, Yaksha's blood. And I began to come back to life. But Eddie vanished before the process was complete, and I was left only half alive." He pauses again. "I assume you destroyed him?"

I nod again. "Yes."

He reaches across the table and takes my hands. His skin is warm, and it quiets the trembles that continue deep inside me. He continues his impossible tale, and I listen because I can do nothing more.

"Still, I continued to gain strength without Eddie's help. In a day—maybe it was two—I was able to move about. I was in a deserted warehouse, tied with rope. I had no trouble breaking out, and when I did I read about all the strange goings on in Las Vegas, and

I knew you must be there." He stops. "It was me who was at the door."

I nod for a fourth time. No wonder the voice sounded familiar. "Why didn't you identify yourself?" I ask.

"I knew you wouldn't believe me until you saw me."

"That's true."

He squeezes my hands. "It's me, Sita. I've come back for you. It's Ray. Why can't you at least smile?"

I try to smile but I just end up shaking my head. "I don't know. You were gone. I knew you were gone. I had no hope." My eyes burn with tears. "And I don't know if I'm not just imagining this."

"You were never one to imagine things."

"But I'm no longer the one you knew." I withdraw my hands from his and clasp them together, trying to hold myself together. "I'm human now. The vampire is dead."

He is not surprised. "You let go of my hands too quickly, Sita. If you examine them, you will notice a change in me as well."

"What do you mean?" I gasp.

"I watched you at that house. I watched you enter it, and I watched you leave it. I knew you were not the same, and I wondered what had happened in there. I explored the house, and found the basement: the copper sheets, the crystals, the magnets, the vial of human blood." He pauses. "I performed the same experiment on myself. I am no longer a vampire either."

The shocks keep piling one on top of the other. I cannot cope. "How did you know what to do?" I whisper.

He shrugs. "What was there to know? The equipment was all set up. I just had to lie down and allow the vibration of the human blood to wash over my aura as the reflected sun shone through the vial of blood." He glances out the window. There is a kind of light in the east. "I did it this afternoon. Now the sunrise will no longer hurt me."

The tears in my eyes travel over my cheeks. My mind travels with them as my disbelief washes away. Swallowing thickly, I finally feel as if my body returns to my control. In a burst I realize I am not imagining anything. Ray is not dead! My love is alive! Now I can live my life! Leaning across the table, I kiss his lips. Then I brush his hair and kiss that as well. And I am happy, more happy than I can remember being in thousands of years.

"It is you," I whisper. "God, how can it be you?"

He laughs. "You have Eddie to thank."

I sit back down in my seat and feel my warm human heart pounding in my chest. My anxiety, my fear, my confusion—all these things have now transformed into a solitary glow of wonder. For a while now I have cursed Krishna for what he has done to me, and now I can only bow inside in gratitude. For I have no doubt Krishna has brought Ray back to me, not that monster Eddie Fender.

"Let's not even speak his name," I say. "I cut off his head and burned his remains. He is gone—he will never return." I pause. "I'm sorry."

He frowns. "What have you to be sorry for?"

"Assuming you were dead." I shrug. "Joel told me you were blown to pieces."

Ray sighs and looks down at his own hands. "He wasn't far wrong." He glances up. "I didn't see Joel at the house?"

My lower lips trembles. "He's dead."

"I'm sorry."

"We both have to stop saying that." I smile a sad smile. "I made him a vampire as well, trying to save him. But it just killed him in the end."

"Who created the equipment that transformed us back into human beings?"

"Arturo—old friend, from the Middle Ages. I was in love with him. He was an alchemist, the greatest who ever lived. He experimented with my blood and changed himself into a hybrid of a vampire and a human. That's how he was able to survive all these years." I lower my voice. "He died with Joel. He had to die."

Ray nods. One didn't have to explain every detail to him in order for him to understand. He knew Arturo must have still been after my blood; that he was dangerous. Ray understood that I could kill those I loved, as I had almost killed him. Ray reaches for my hand again.

"You have blood on you," he says. "Surely you're not still thirsty?"

"No, it's not like you think." I speak in a whisper. "Two men attacked me at the beach. I had to kill them."

"How?"

"I shot them in the head."

Now it is Ray's turn to be shocked. "We have to get out of here, away from here. Besides the government, you'll have the police after you too." He glances toward the door of the coffee shop. "I know you have Seymour with you."

I understand what he wants to say. "I have told him he has to go home."

"He won't want to leave you. You'll have to leave him."

"I have been thinking about that. I just don't know how to explain it to him."

Ray is sympathetic, but a curious note enters his voice. For a moment he sounds like I used to as the pragmatist.

"Don't explain it to him," he says. "Just leave him, and don't tell him where you're going."

"That seems harsh."

"No. You of all people know that to keep him with you will be harsh. You'll expose him to danger for no reason." He softens his tone. "You know I speak from experience."

"You're right. He's asleep at the hotel right now. I suppose I can sneak in, grab my things, and be away before he wakes up." But inside I know I will at least leave him a note. "Where are we going?"

It is Ray's turn to lean over and kiss me. "Sita, we can go anywhere we want. We can do anything we want." He whispers in my ear. "We can even get married and start a family if you want."

I have to laugh, and cry as well. My happiness lingers like the warmth of the sun after a perfect summer day. It is the winter outside, the darkness, that seems the illusion.

"I would like a daughter," I whisper, holding him close.

4 ~——

Two months later we are in Whittier, a suburb of Los
Angeles, where the late President Nixon attended
college. The city is largely middle class, completely
nondescript, a perfect place, in Ray's opinion, to
disappear. Certainly I have never been to Whittier
before, nor harbored any secret desires to go there. We
rent a plain three-bedroom house not far from a
boring mall. Ray picked it out. There is a large
backyard and an olive tree in the front yard. We buy a
second-hand car and purchase our groceries at a Vons
down the street. I have lived five thousand years to do
all these things.

Yet my happiness has not faded with the passage of
the eight weeks. Sleeping beside Ray, walking with
him in the morning, sitting beside him in a movie—

these simple acts mean more to me than all the earth-shattering deeds I have accomplished since I was conceived beneath Yaksha's bloody bite. It is all because I am human, I know, and in love. How young love makes me feel. How lovely are all humans. Shopping at the mall, in the grocery store, I often find myself stopping to stare at people. For too long I admired them, despised them, and envied them, and now I am one of them. The hard walls of my universe have collapsed. Now I see the sun rise and feel the space beyond it, not just the emptiness. The pain in my heart, caused by the burning stake, has finally healed. The void in my chest has been filled.

Especially when I discover that I am pregnant.

It happens the early morning of the full moon, two months after the nuclear bomb detonated in the desert beneath a previous full moon. A fifteen-dollar early pregnancy kit tells me the good news. I shake the blue test tube in the bathroom and Ray comes running when I let out a loud cry. What is the matter, he wants to know? I am shaking—there must be something wrong. I don't even get a chance to show him my blue urine because I accidentally spill it all over him. He gets the picture and laughs with me, and at me.

I am at the bookstore later the same day, browsing through the baby books, when I meet Paula Ramirez. A pretty young woman of twenty-five, she has long black hair as shiny as her smooth complexion and a belly larger than her enchanting brown eyes. Obviously she is expecting, much sooner than I am. I smile at her as she juggles six different baby books in one arm, while reaching for another with her free hand.

"You know," I say. "Women were having kids long before there were books. It's a natural process." I put my own book back on the shelf. "Anyway, I don't think any of these authors know what the hell they're talking about."

She nods at my remark. "Are you pregnant?"

"Yes. And so are you, unless I'm blind." I offer my hand, and because I like her, without even knowing her, I tell her one of my more real names. Even as a human, I often trust my intuition. "I'm Alisa."

She shakes my hand. "Paula. How far along are you?"

"I don't know. I haven't even been to the doctor. It can't be more than two months, though, unless God is the father."

For some reason, Paula loses her smile. "Do you live around here?"

"Yes. Close enough to walk to the mall. How about you?"

"I'm on Grove," Paula says. "You know where that is?"

"Just around the block from us."

Paula hesitates. "Forgive me for asking, but are you married?"

It is a curious question, but I'm not offended. "No. But I live with my boyfriend. Are you married?"

Sorrow touches her face. "No." She pats her big belly. "I have to take care of this one alone." She adds, "I work at St. Andrews. It's just down the block from where you live."

"I have seen the crucifix. What do you do at St. Andrews?"

"I am supposed to be an assistant to the Mother Superior but I end up doing whatever's necessary. That includes scrubbing the bathroom floors, if no one's gotten to them. The church and the high school operate on a tight budget." She adds, almost by way of apology, "But I take frequent breaks. I pray a lot."

For some reason this girl interests me. She has special qualities—a gentleness of manner, a kindness in her voice. She is not a big girl but she seems to take up a lot of space. What I mean is there is a presence about her. Yet she acts anything but powerful, and that I also like.

"What do you pray for?" I ask.

Paula smiles shyly and lowers her head. "I shouldn't say."

I pat her on the back. "That's all right, you don't have to tell me. Who knows? Prayers could be like wishes. Maybe they lose their magic if you talk about them."

Paula studies me. "Where are you from, Alisa?"

"Up north. Why?"

"I could swear I've seen you before."

Her remark touches me deeply. Because in that exact moment, I feel the same way. There is something familiar in her eyes, in the soft light of their dark depths. They remind me of, well, the past, and I still have much of that, even if I grow older with each day.

Yet I intend to brush her comment aside, as I brush aside thoughts of my own mortality that come in the middle of night, when Ray is asleep beside me, and sleep is hard to find. My insomnia is the only obvious curse of my transformation. I must still be used to hunting in the middle of the night. Prowling the streets in a black leather miniskirt. Death with a sexy smile and an endless thirst. Now, instead, I get up from bed and have a glass of warm milk and say my prayers—to Krishna, of course, whom I believe was God. I still remember him best during the darkest hours.

Krishna was once asked what was the most miraculous thing in all of creation, and he replied, "That a man should wake each morning and believe deep in his heart that he will live forever, even though he knows that he is doomed to die." Despite my many human weaknesses, a part of me still feels as if I will never die. And that part has never felt so alive as when I stare at Paula, a simple pregnant young woman that I have met by chance in a mall bookstore.

"I just have one of those faces," I reply.

We have lunch, and I get to know Paula better, and I let her know a few censored facts about myself. By the time our food is finished, we are fast friends, and this I see as a positive step on my road to becoming truly human. We exchange numbers and promise to stay in touch, and I know we will. I like Paula—really; it is almost as if I have a crush on her, though I have had few female lovers during my fifty centuries, and certainly Ray now takes care of all my sexual needs. It is just that as I say goodbye to her, I am already thinking of the next time we will meet, and how nice it will be.

Paula is the rarest of human beings. Someone with intelligence and humility. It has been my observation that the more intelligent a man or woman is, the more dishonest he or she is. Modern psychologists, I know, would not agree with me, but they are often dishonest themselves. Psychology has never impressed me as a science. Who has ever really defined the mind, much less the heart? Paula has a quick mind that has not destroyed her innocence. As we part for the first time, she insists on paying for our meal even when it is clear she has little money. But I let her pay since it seems to mean a lot to her.

5 ~~~~

And so, for a week, life went on, sweetly, smoothly, with a new friend, a reborn lover, and a baby growing inside me. A daughter, I am sure, even though I pray to God to make it an absolute certainty. Yet fifty centuries cannot be forgotten. History cannot be rewritten. I live in the suburbs and abide by my country's laws. I have a new library card and am thinking of buying a little dog. Yet I have murdered thousands, tens of thousands, brutally and without mercy. That is a bloody fact, and perhaps there is such a thing as karma, of sin and judgment. I wonder if I am being judged when I begin to have trouble with the baby.

It is not normal trouble.

It is the worst kind. The supernatural kind.

The baby is growing much faster than she should. As I said to Paula, I can only be two months pregnant, and yet, one week after I meet Paula, I wake with something kicking in my abdomen. After hurrying to the bathroom and turning on the light—for I cannot see very well in the dark anymore—I am astounded to see that my stomach bulges through my nightgown. In the space of hours, even, the baby has developed through an entire trimester. This does not please me.

"Ray," I say. "Ray!"

He comes running, and takes forever to see what the problem is. Finally he puts his hand on my belly. "This is not normal?"

"Are you nuts?" I brush his hand aside. "She can't be human."

"We're human," he says.

"Are we?" I ask the empty bathtub.

He puts a hand on my shoulder. "This accelerated growth doesn't have to be a bad thing."

I am having trouble breathing. I had put so much hope in the past being past. But there is no future, not really. It is only a phantom of what we want to deny, a dream in a time that will never actually be.

"Anything abnormal is bad," I say. "Especially when you have to answer yes to the question on the medical form: Have you ever been a vampire?"

"The child cannot be a vampire," Ray says simply. "Vampires cannot reproduce this way."

"You mean they haven't done so in the past," I say. "When has a vampire ever turned human again? This is new terrain." I lean over and spit in the sink. My spit is bloody—I bit my lower lip the instant the light went on. "It's an omen," I say.

Ray rubs my back. "Maybe you should see a doctor. You were going to start looking for one anyway."

I chuckle bitterly. "I cannot see a doctor. We're in hiding, remember? Doctors report local monsters to the authorities. Young women who have babies in three months." The baby kicks again. I stare in the mirror at my bulge. "If it even takes that long."

My words prove prophetic. Over the next four days the baby grows at an insane pace, a month of development for each twenty-four-hour period. During this time I am forced to eat and drink constantly, but seldom do I have to use the rest room. Red meat, in particular, I crave. I have three hamburgers for breakfast and in the evening four New York steaks, washed down with quarts of Evian. Still, I burn with hunger, with thirst, and with fear. What would an ultrasound show? A horned harlot grinning back at the sound waves?

During this time, I avoid Paula and the world. Ray is my only companion. He holds my hand and says little. What is there to say? Time will tell all.

Five days after waking in the middle of the night to see my swollen belly, I awake again in the early morning hours in horrible pain with cramps in my abdomen. Just before Ray wakes, I remember when I had my first child, five thousand years earlier. My dear Lalita—she who plays. That birth had been painless, ecstatic even. I had intended to name this child by the same name. But as another spasm grips me, seemingly threatening to rip me in two, I don't know if such a gentle title will be appropriate. I sit up gasping for air.

"Oh God," I whisper.

Ray stirs beside me. His voice is calm. "Is it time?"

"It's time."

"Do you want to go to the hospital?"

We have discussed this, but never come to a decision. I can withstand tremendous physical pain, and of course I have delivered babies many times and know human anatomy inside out. Yet this pain is a thing of demons. It transcends any form of torment I have ever experienced. Literally, I feel as if I am being ripped apart, consumed from the inside. What is my child doing to me? I bury my face in my hands.

"It feels like it's eating my womb," I moan.

Ray is on his feet. "We have to get help. We have to risk the hospital."

"No." I grab his hand as he reaches for the car keys. "I won't make it. It's coming too fast."

He kneels at my side. "But I don't know what to do."

I fight for air. "It doesn't matter. It's all being done."

"Should I call for Paula?" Ray approves of my relationship with Paula, although, for some strange reason, he has avoided meeting her. How I long for her company right then, her soothing smile. Yet I know she is the last person who should see me like this. I shake my head and feel the sweat pour off my face.

"No," I say. "This would terrify her. We have to face this alone."

"Should I boil some water?"

For some reason his remark amuses me. "Yes, yes. Boil some water. We can put the baby in it when she comes out." I snort when I see his stunned expression. "That's a joke, Ray."

Yet he stares at me strangely. He speaks to me as if he is speaking to a third person in the room. "Sometimes I feel I came back just for this baby. I don't want anything to happen to her."

Another spasm grips me, and I double up and ignore his serious tone. The agony angers me. "If anything is going to happen to anyone," I whisper, "it will happen to me."

"Sita?"

"Get the goddamn water."

My daughter is born fifteen minutes later, and she puts a nice rip in me as she comes into the world. My blood is everywhere, even in my hair, and I know I am in danger of hemorrhaging to death. It is only now I let Ray call for an ambulance. But before he gets on the phone, he puts my bloody child on my chest. He has already cut the umbilical cord with a sterilized knife from the kitchen drawer. Cuddling my daughter as I lie on the verge of blacking out, I stare into her dark blue eyes and she stares back at me. She does not cry nor make any other sound. For the moment I am just relieved she is breathing.

Yet there is an alertness in her eyes that disturbs me. She looks at me as if she can see me, and all the books say a child of five minutes cannot even focus. Not only that, she stares at me as if she knows me, and the funny thing is, I do likewise. I do know her, and she is not the soul of my gentle and joyful Lalita returned to me from the ancient past. She is someone else, someone, I feel, they may have constructed temples to long ago, when mankind was closer to the gods in heaven and the forgotten creatures beneath the earth. I shiver as I look at her, yet I hold her tight. Her name just springs from my cracked and bleeding lips—I do not bring it forth consciously. The name is a mantra, a prayer, and also a name for that which cannot be named.

"Kalika," I call her. Kali Ma.

Not she who plays. She who destroys.

Still, I love her more than can be said.

6

Kalika is two weeks old, really a year in size and ability, when she refuses to take my milk. For the last fourteen days I have enjoyed feeding her, although I have not relished the speed at which she grows. Each morning when I wake to her sounds, I find a different and older daughter. This morning she pushes me away as I try to hold her to my breast. She is strong and actually bruises my skin as she refuses what I have to offer. Ray sits across from me and tries to comfort me in my despair.

"Maybe she's not feeling well," he says.

I stare out the window as Kalika squirms on my lap. "Maybe she wants something else to drink," I say.

"She's not a vampire."

"You don't know."

"But sunlight doesn't bother her."

It is true, I have tested my daughter under the bright sun. She just stares at it as she stares at everything else. Indeed, the glare does not seem to annoy her young eyes, a fact that does nothing to comfort me.

"No one knows what she is," I say.

"Well, what are we going to do? We have to feed her."

Maybe Kalika understands the question. Already she has begun to speak, simple words as many twelve-month-old children do. But it is probable she understands more than she says, certainly more about herself than either of her parents is willing to admit. While I am gazing out the window at the sky, she leans over and bites my left nipple. She has teeth now and she bites so hard that she draws blood. The pain, for me, is sharp, but the flow, for her, is steady. And the blood seems to satisfy her.

I look at Ray and want to cry.

Another day has gone by and Kalika is in her bedroom screaming. She is hungry but my breasts are too sore—too drained actually—to give her another feeding. Ray paces in front of me as I lie on the living room couch and stare out the big window. My thoughts are often of the sky, and of Krishna. I wonder where God is at times like this, if he is not browsing in the horror section of the cosmic library searching for another chapter to slip in my life story.

I am exhausted—I have yet to regain my strength from the delivery. I'm a smashed doll who's been sewn together by an emotionless doctor, an aching mother whose daughter disembowels Barbies in search of something to eat. Kalika lets out another loud cry and Ray shakes his head in disgust.

"What are we going to do?" he asks.

"You asked me that five minutes ago."

"Well, we've got to do something. A child's got to eat."

"I offered her a steak, a raw steak even, and she didn't want it. I offered her the blood from the steak and she didn't want it. She just wants my blood and if I give her any more I will die." I cough weakly. "But considering the circumstance that might not be bad."

Ray stops pacing and stares down at me. "Maybe she doesn't just crave *your* blood."

I speak in a flat voice. "I have thought of that. I would have to be stupid not to have thought of that." I pause. "Do you want to give her some of your blood?"

Ray kneels on the floor beside me. He takes my hand and gives it an affectionate squeeze. But there is a look in his eyes, one I have never seen before. Of course having a child like Kalika in the house would give the Pope a new look. Ray speaks in a low conspiratorial voice and there is no affection in his words.

"Let us say she is not a human being," he admits. "I suppose that is obvious by now. Let's even go so far as to say she's some sort of vampire, although not a vampire in the traditional sense. Her indifference to the sun makes that seem certain. Now, all of this is not necessarily a bad thing if we can teach her right from wrong as she matures. She doesn't have to be a monster."

"What's your point?"

"Isn't it obvious? She's still our daughter. We still love her, and we have to give her what she needs to survive, at least until she can fend for herself." He pauses. "We have to get her fresh blood."

I smile without pleasure. "You mean we have to get her fresh victims."

"We just need blood, for now. We don't have to kill anyone to get it."

"Fine. Go down to the hospital and buy some. Take one of my credit cards. They're in my purse on the kitchen table."

Ray drew back. "I'm serious, Sita."

I chuckle bitterly. "So am I. I have experience in these matters, in case you've forgotten. The only blood she will take will be warm blood from a human being."

"I thought you sometimes survived on animal blood."

"I offered her the blood of a cat I caught and killed in the backyard and she didn't want it."

"You didn't tell me."

"Killing a cat wasn't something I felt like bragging about."

A peculiar note enters his voice, to match the strange look in his eyes. "You used to kill people all the time."

I brush off his hand and sit up. "Is that what you want me to do? Murder people for her?"

"No. No one has to die. You told me that the day you made me a vampire."

My temper flares. "The day I made you a vampire I had an arsenal of supernatural powers at my command. I could lure dozens of people into my lair, and let them go with little more than a headache. To get Kalika fresh blood, I will have to kill, and that I refuse to do now."

"Now that you're human?"

"Yes. Now that I'm human. And don't remind me of those two I wasted the night you returned. That was an act of self-defense."

"This is an act of self-preservation," Rays says.

I speak impatiently. "How am I supposed to get someone to donate blood for Kalika's breakfast? Where do you find people like that? Not in Whittier."

"Where did you go to find victims before? To bars? You went to them to lure men back to your place."

"I never took them back to my place."

Ray hesitates. "But we need someone, maybe a couple of someones we can take blood from regularly."

I snicker. "Yeah, right. And when we let them go we just tell them to please not mention what has been going on here. Just chalk the bloodletting off to a unique experience." I fume. "Whoever we bring here, we'll have to kill in the end. I won't do that."

"Then you'll let your daughter die?"

I glare at Ray, searching for the loving young man I once knew. "What's happened to you? You should be on the other side of this argument. Before the blast, you would have been. Where did you go when you died? Huh? You never told me. Was it hell? Did the devil teach you a few new tricks?"

He is offended. "I'm just trying to save our daughter. I wish you'd drop your self-righteous, pompous attitude and face the facts—Kalika needs blood or she will die. We have to get her blood."

"Fine, go out and get a young woman victim. You're handsome and you've got style. It shouldn't take you long."

He stops. "I don't know how to pick up people. I've never done it before."

I have to laugh. "You sure picked me up easily enough."

Kalika screams again.

Ray loses his dark expression and looks pained. "Please," he says. "She's all we've got. You're the only one who can save her."

Fed up with arguing, I stand and grab my black leather coat, the one I used to wear for hunting. Heading for the door, I say over my shoulder, "We used to have a lot, Ray. Remember that next time you order me to go out and kill."

7

I drive around for an hour before ending up at a local park. There are a couple of basketball courts, a baseball diamond, a circular pond with white ducks in it, and a wide field where children fly long-tailed kites. Sitting between the pond and the basketball courts, I try to think how I can fix my miserable life in one brilliant stroke.

For the last twenty-four hours I have considered taking Kalika to Arturo's secret laboratory, where the paraphernalia that completed my transformation is located: the crucifix-shaped magnets, the long copper sheets, the colored crystals. Yet the attempt, I know, to make Kalika into a human, would be a desperate act at best. One of the few times Arturo experimented on a boy—dear Ralphe—the results were disastrous.

Ralphe was transformed into a flesh-eating ghoul, and I had to break his neck with my own hands to stop him from killing. No, I realize, I cannot experiment on Kalika, not until every other alternative has been explored.

Which means I need human blood. Now.

A young man on the basketball court glances over at me. I may not be a vampire anymore, but I know I'm cute. This guy is maybe nineteen, with blond hair and a strong build, an easy six-two. His size is important to me. The more pounds he has, the more blood he can stand to lose. Yet the more difficult he will be to contain. But my daughter is screaming at home. I heard her screams as I drove away in the car, echoing in my ears like the cries of a thousand past victims.

I catch this young man's eye and smile.

He flashes me a grin. He is interested, doomed.

When his game finishes, he strolls over to say hi.

"Hi," I say in response, nodding to the court, to his companions. I sit with my profile to them—I don't want them to get a good look at me. "You know, you're pretty good. You have a great jump shot."

"Thanks. I still enjoy these pick-up games."

"You used to play in high school?"

"Yeah. Just got out last year. How about you?"

I laugh softly. "I was too short to play basketball."

He blushes. "I mean, did you just graduate?"

"Not long ago." I pause, let my eyes slide over him. "What's your name?"

"Eric Hawkins. What's yours?"

I stand and offer him my hand. "Cynthia Rhodes. Do you come here often?"

"I usually play at Centinela. This park—I haven't been here in ages."

That's good, I think. "What brings you here today?"

He shrugs. "Nothing in particular. I was just out driving around."

That's also good. The other guys he's playing with—they're not close friends.

"I was just doing the same," I say.

He glances at the ground, fidgets shyly. "Hey, would you like to go have a Coke or something?"

"Sure. I'm not doing anything."

We go to a coffee shop, and I order coffee. I have become a big coffee drinker since becoming human. It does wonders for my insomnia. Eric has a hamburger and french fries. I am happy he eats heartily. He will need his strength. Yet as he talks about himself, I begin to feel sad. He seems like such a nice boy.

"I'm taking a year off from college, but I'll be in school next year," he says. "I just got accepted to SC. I'm going to major in pre-med. My old man's a doctor and he's encouraged me to follow in his footsteps since the day I learned to talk."

"Why didn't you go straight to college?"

"I wanted to travel a little, work a little. I spent the summer in Europe. Spent a month in the Greek islands alone. You ever been there?"

I nod as I sip my coffee. "Yes. Did you visit Delos?"

"The island with all the ruins?"

"Yes. It's supposed to be the most sacred island in

the Aegean Sea. Apollo was born there." I lower my voice. "At least, that's what the stories say."

"Yeah, I was there. When were you there?"

"A few years back." I pause and catch his eye, and hate myself for the blatant manipulation. "I'm glad I went to the park today."

He smiles shyly and stares down at his hamburger. "Yeah. When I saw you sitting there all by yourself—I don't know—I just felt like I had to talk to you." He adds, "I don't usually go around hitting on girls."

"I know, Eric."

We chat a while longer and he finishes his food, and then glances at his watch. "Boy, I better get going. My dad's expecting me at his office. I help out there Tuesday and Thursday afternoons."

I feel a moment of panic. I cannot imagine returning to Kalika's screams empty-handed. Reaching across the table, I touch his hand. "Could you do me a quick favor?"

"Sure. What is it?"

"It's kind of embarrassing to explain. You see, I have this ex-boyfriend who is sort of stalking me. He's not violent or anything like that, but if he sees me return home he immediately jumps out of his car and runs over and starts hassling me." I pause. "Could you follow me home in your car? Just to make sure I get in OK." I add, "I don't live far from here."

"You don't live with your parents?"

"No. Both my parents are dead. I live alone."

Eric is troubled. "Sure, I can come. But I won't be able to stay."

"I understand. If you can just walk me to my door."

Eric is agreeable, although his reluctance remains. As a human, I'm not the actress I used to be. He likes me, but he is slightly suspicious of me. I have to wonder exactly what I'm going to do with him once he's in my house.

To my immense bad luck, Paula is standing on my front porch as I drive up and park. Waving to her, I quickly run back to Eric's car, which is in the middle of the block. I ask if he can wait a minute, but he's anxious to get to his father's office.

"He loses his temper if I'm even ten minutes late," he explains.

"I'm grateful you followed me this far," I say. "But I'm still worried my ex is around. He could even be in the house."

Eric nods to Paula, who waits patiently for me. "Who is she?"

I snort, and feel another layer of guilt. "She's just this pregnant girl who stops by from time to time looking for money. I have to get rid of her, or she'll stay all afternoon." I touch his arm. "Please stay. Give me two minutes."

Eric hesitates. "OK."

Paula flashes me a warm smile as I hurry toward her. "What are you doing here?" I ask.

"I was worried about you. I haven't heard from you in so long." Paula studies me, and I know how perceptive she is. "Have you been sick? You look pale."

"I've had a bad flu. Look, I can't talk right now. That guy in the car—he's my boyfriend's brother, and he's in deep trouble that I can't go into right now. He needs my help."

Paula is hesitant. "Fine, I can go. I was just out for a walk." She glances at Eric. "Are you sure you're all right?"

"Yeah, no problem." I gesture to her swollen belly. "It won't be long now."

Paula is radiant. "No. Another three weeks is all."

"That's great." I nod to my door. "Did you knock? Did you talk to Ray?"

"I knocked but no one answered."

"Oh." That's strange. Ray is almost always at home. He would have to be at home, with Kalika and all. I can't imagine him taking her out. But perhaps our daughter is the reason he didn't answer. I cannot hear either of them inside. I add, "I'll talk to you soon, Paula. I promise, we'll have lunch."

Paula is gracious as she carefully moves down the steps. "You take care. I'll be thinking of you."

"Thanks. Say a prayer for me."

"I always do, Alisa."

Paula leaves, and I gesture for Eric to join me on the front porch. He parks in my driveway and approaches reluctantly. He has antennae of his own. I am definitely giving off bad vibes. His car will have to be moved quickly, I think, before if makes an impression on my neighbors. I fumble for my keys, like I'm nervous. And I am nervous—I can't imagine hurting him. For that matter, he might end up hurting me.

"Sometimes my ex comes in a back window," I say as I put the key in the lock.

"You should lock your windows," Eric mutters.

"Can I get you something to drink?" I ask as we step inside. A quick look around shows neither Ray nor Kalika. Maybe he did go out with her. Eric stays near the door.

"I really should be going," he says.

"At least have a lemonade. I made some fresh this morning." I move toward the kitchen. "I really appreciate you doing this for me."

Eric feels trapped. "I'll have a small glass," he says without enthusiasm.

In fact, I did make lemonade that morning, from concentrate. Pouring a couple of glasses, I hurry back to the living room. My resentment toward Ray continues to grow. For seducing Eric to come into the house, it is good Ray is out of sight. Yet I could use Ray to knock Eric unconscious. I mean, I am a hundred-and-ten pound blond chick who just had a baby. Eric accepts his drink and I toast him with our glasses. Eric drinks without relish.

"It's good," he mumbles.

"Thanks. We have lemon trees in our backyard."

"They give fruit this time of year?"

I smile. "No, but they do in the summer."

Eric finishes half his drink and sets the glass down on the coffee table. "Well, my dad's waiting. Let's talk another time. It was nice to meet you."

I jump slightly, and speak in a hushed tone. "Did you hear that?"

Eric is puzzled. "What?"

I point down the hall. "I think he's here."

Eric frowns. "I don't hear anything."

I am a picture of fear. "Would you check? Just to be sure."

"Cynthia, really. I don't think anyone's there."

I swallow heavily. "Please? It's terrible when he sneaks up on me like this. I can't get rid of him by myself."

Eric eyes the hallway. "You're sure he's not violent? Why does he break into your house?"

"He's never violent. He's just a pest. I hope I'm imagining the whole thing."

Eric starts up the hallway. I follow close behind him, silently. Even as a human, I can move like a cat. As he reaches for the last bedroom door on the left, I lash out with my right foot, striking behind his right knee. There is a mushy tearing sound—the spot is especially vulnerable. Letting out a painful cry, Eric topples to his knees. Before he can recover, I slash out with my left hand and catch him in the left temple, which is the thinnest part of the skull. The blow stuns him but does not knock him out. Disgusted, I strike again, at the opposite temple, hitting as hard as I can, the side of my hand throbbing from the effort. Still on his knees, he sways precariously. Yet he refuses to go down. Quite the contrary, he grasps at the near wall, trying to pull himself up. He is a fighter and it breaks my heart not to let him go. But I'm committed now. Backing up a step, I jump in the air and kick him in the back of the head with the heel of my left boot. That does the trick. Eric falls forward like a sack of flour. Blood drips off the back of his head, staining the carpet. Just what we need.

"I'm sorry," I whisper as I kneel by his side,

checking the pulse at the side of his neck to make sure I haven't killed him. His face against the floor, Eric breathes heavily but his pulse is strong.

Suddenly I am aware of someone at my back.

"Good job," Ray says.

I turn on him angrily. "Yeah, it's good I was able to handle him all by myself. Where have you been?"

He shrugs. "I was in the other room."

"Where's Kalika?"

He nods to the door Eric was about to open. "In there. I told her to remain silent."

"And she listened to you?"

Ray speaks seriously. "She always listens to me."

"Lucky you." I nod to Eric. "Where are we going to put him?"

"In the spare room. We'll tie him up and gag him, and take only as much blood as our daughter needs."

"That might be more than he can give," I say, stroking Eric's hair.

"We'll have to worry about that later." Ray pauses. "How should we withdraw the blood?"

"We need needles, syringes, tourniquets, tubing, flasks. I have them at my house in Beverly Hills." I stand, wiping Eric's blood from my hands. "I'll go now."

Ray stops me. "That house might be watched, you said."

I don't like being stopped. "I'll have to risk it. I'm not breaking into a drugstore to get this stuff."

"I want you to help me tie him up before you leave."

"Can't you tie him up? The sooner I leave, the

sooner I can get back." I glance at the bedroom door. My daughter hasn't made a peep. "Kalika must be starving by now."

"It won't take us long if we work together. Then I can go with you to the other house."

"No," I say. "I'm going alone."

Ray hesitates. "Fine. But I think it's better this guy sees only one of us."

"Why?"

"Isn't it obvious? If he can identify me, it doubles our chances of being caught."

I stare at Ray. "You really have changed."

He shrugs. "Maybe it was Eddie's blood."

"Maybe." I hold his eye. "All right, I'll deal with him, like I deal with everything else. As long as we both understand that we're not pushing Eric beyond his limit. This boy is not going to die."

Ray nods his head, but his eyes do not seem to agree.

8 ～～～

Before entering my Beverly Hills house, I search the street and the surrounding houses for signs of anyone watching. The FBI's methods are not unfamiliar to me. The house appears unwatched. Once inside, I gather the supplies I need to turn Eric into a serious anemic. But before leaving I stop to call Seymour. I haven't spoken to him since I said good night in the hotel by the beach. Even the note I left said little.

Sorry, Seymour. Got to go. You know this is for the best. Love, Sita.

"Hello?" he says.

"It's me."

He takes a long time to answer. His voice comes out harsh. "What do you want?"

I speak with sincerity. "Just to hear your voice, Seymour. I miss you."

"Yeah, right."

"I do. I really do."

"Where are you?"

"I can't tell you."

"I have to go."

"No! Wait! You know why I can't tell you."

"No, I don't know why. I thought you were my friend. Friends don't leave each other in the middle of the night." He lowers his voice and there is pain in it. "Why did you leave?"

I hesitate. I didn't plan to tell him.

"Ray's come back."

Seymour is astounded. "That's impossible."

"It's true. We're living together." I add, "We've got a daughter."

"Sita, what kind of fool do you think I am? You haven't had time to have a daughter."

My voice cracks. "I know that. But this one came rather fast."

He hears that I'm serious. "Tell me everything that's happened since I last saw you."

So I tell him because I need someone to talk to. As always he listens patiently, closely, and I have to wonder what insights he will provide when I'm finished. He's so smart—he always has something interesting to say about my numerous predicaments. Yet the next words out of his mouth shock me.

"Why do you assume this guy is Ray?" he asks when I finish.

I have to laugh, although I almost choke on it.

"What kind of question is that? Of course it's Ray. I know it's Ray. Who else could it be?"

"I don't know who else it could be. But how do you know it's Ray? Remember, he died."

"Because he looks like Ray. He acts like Ray. He knows everything Ray knew. He can't be an impostor."

Seymour speaks calmly. "Let's take each of your statements. He looks like Ray you say. OK, I grant you that because you've seen him and I haven't. But you say he acts like Ray? I don't think so. The Ray you describe isn't the Ray I remember."

"He's been through a lot. In a sense, he died during the blast. It was only Eddie's blood that brought him back to life."

"That worries me right there. Eddie was the incarnation of evil. What would his blood do to someone's psyche? Even the psyche of another vampire?"

I close my eyes and sigh. "I've worried about that myself. But please believe me, he can't be an impostor. Dozens of times we've discussed things only Ray and I knew."

"But you do accept you're dealing with a guy that has his priorities twisted?"

"Am I? I've asked myself that question many times. When you get right down to it, I would do anything to save Kalika. Ray's her father. Is he so different from me?"

"I don't know. There's something in your story—something I can't put my finger on. I think Ray's dangerous, and I'd keep an eye on him. But let's leave that for a moment. Let's talk about Kalika. How can she be a vampire and not be sensitive to the sun?"

"I wasn't that sensitive," I say.

"Because you'd been a vampire for over five thousand years. And still the sun did bother you; it sapped your strength. You say it doesn't affect her at all?"

"Not as far as I can tell. She plays out in it."

"Does she make any effort to move into the shade?"

"No. She likes the sun as much as the moon."

"Yet she wants human blood," Seymour muttered, thinking aloud. "Hmm. Is she exceptionally strong?"

"Yes. Pretty strong. She must be a vampire."

Seymour considers. "What does she look like?"

"A lot like me, except her features are darker."

"You mean she has brown hair, brown eyes?"

"Her hair is brown, but her eyes are a dark blue." I add painfully, "She's very pretty. You'd like her."

"Not if she wants to drink my blood. Sita, let's be frank with each other. You're not superhuman anymore. You're not going to be able to go around abducting people without getting caught. As far as I can tell, you were lucky with this Eric guy. And how are you going to let him go when you're through with him? He'll go straight to the police."

I bite my lower lip and taste the blood. The flavor gives me no strength.

"I know," I say.

"If you know then you've got to stop now."

There are tears pooled in my eyes but I won't shed them. Not tonight. "I can't, Seymour. Ray's right about one thing. I can't let her die."

Seymour speaks gently. "You know what I'm going to ask next."

I nod weakly. "Yes. Does the world need a monster like her? All I can say is, I'm hoping she turns out all right. For godsakes, she was just born. She hasn't had a chance to show what she's like."

"But by the time she does, it might be too late. You might not be able to stop her." He adds carefully, "But you can stop her now."

I'm aghast. "I can't murder my own daughter!"

"You can stop feeding her. Think what those feedings will cost you and your victims. You'll need a dozen Erics to keep her satisfied if she's growing at the rate you say. In fact, she'll be getting her own Erics soon enough. I know this is painful for you to face, but you should probably end it now."

I shake my head vigorously. "I can't do that."

Seymour is sympathetic. "But then I can't help you." He adds, "Unless you tell me where you are."

"It won't help for you to see her. You'll just fall in love with her. When she's not hungry, she's really very lovely."

"I was thinking I'd like to speak to this new and improved Ray."

"I don't think that's a good idea. Not now."

Seymour speaks with feeling. "You've trusted me in the past, Sita. Trust me now. You're too close to this. You can't see what's real. You need me."

"It's too dangerous, Seymour. If something happened to you, I'd never forgive myself. Stay where you are, I'll call you again. And I'll think about what you've said."

"Thinking won't stop her from growing into what she really is."

"I suppose we'll see what that is soon enough."

We exchange goodbyes. As I leave the house, I think of Eddie Fender's blood circulating in my lover's body. And I wonder what blood pumps through Kalika's veins. What it is capable of doing.

9

At home, Eric has regained consciousness. His feet and hands are firmly bound, and there is duct tape over his mouth, but he has somehow managed to squirm his way so that he is sitting upright in the far corner of the spare bedroom. His eyes are wide with fear as I approach him with a syringe. It is hard to blame him. As I kneel by his side, I start to stroke his head but he trembles under my fingers so I stop.

"I'm sorry," I say. "This isn't easy for me either. I wish I could explain the whole situation to you but I can't. But I can promise you that you're not going to die. I swear this to you, Eric, and I keep my word. At the same time, I'm going to have to keep you here for a few days. I'm not exactly sure how long. And while you're here—please don't freak out over this—I'm going to have to occasionally take some of your blood."

The last sentence does not go over well. Eric's eyes get so round I'm afraid they're going to burst from his skull. He shakes his head violently from side to side and tries to wiggle away. But I pull him back.

"Shh," I say. "It's not going to be as bad as it sounds. I have clean needles, and am better trained than most doctors. You can lose a little blood and it won't damage you in the slightest."

He works his mouth vigorously. His meaning is clear.

"If I remove your gag," I say, "will you promise not to scream? If you do scream, I'll have to shut you up quickly, and I don't want to have to hurt you any more than I have to."

Eric nods rapidly.

"OK. But you mustn't raise your voice." I tear off the tape. Ouch.

Eric gasps for air. "Who are you?" he moans pitifully.

"Well, that's an interesting question. I am not Cynthia Rhodes if that's what you're asking, but I suppose you know that already." I pause. "I'm just a stranger in the park."

"What do you want with me?"

"I told you. Your blood. A little of your blood."

"But what do you want my blood for?" he cries.

"That's a long story." I pat him on the shoulder. "Just trust me that I really need it, and that in the end you're going to be OK."

He is breathing heavily. He stares down at his leg

and looks so pitiful it breaks my heart. "You broke my knee. It hurts. I need a doctor."

"I'm sorry. You can see a doctor later, in a few days. But until then you'll have to stay here. You'll have to eat here, and sleep here, and go to the bathroom here. Now you see that bathroom over there? I will let you use it from time to time if you just cooperate with me. In fact, if you're real good, I won't have to keep you tied up at all. You'll be able to walk around this room, even read and listen to music. But I warn you, I'm going to board up all the windows as soon as I take care of other business. And if you do try to escape, well, let's just say that wouldn't be a good idea."

He is a little slow. "Would you kill me?"

I nod gravely. "I would kill you slowly, Eric, by draining away all your blood. It's not a pleasant way to die. So don't mess with me." I fluff up his hair. "Now stick out your arm and don't move."

He tries to back up. "No!"

"Don't raise your voice."

"No!"

I ram the heel of my palm into his nose, which stuns him. While he tries to refocus his eyes, I replace the duct tape and grab his arm. I have the tourniquet on in seconds. His veins are big and bulging. Before he can pull away, I have a needle in his vein and blood flowing into a sterile tube. I lean over and whisper in his ear.

"Don't fight me," I say. "If you force me to hit you again, it won't be in the face, but in a much more sensitive spot." I tug on his earlobe. "Understand?"

He stares at the tube as his blood drips into it. He nods.

"Good boy." I kiss his cheek. "Just think of all this as a nightmare that will soon be over."

Kalika is waiting in the living room with Ray when I bring out the blood in a flask. She has a book on her lap. I assume it is one of the picture books that I have recently bought for her, but I am mistaken. Sitting beside her on the floor, I see she has been paging through an anatomy textbook that was in the house when we rented it. I don't ask if she knows what it is. I'm afraid that she might. Her dark blue eyes brighten when she sees the blood. Her little hands shoot out.

"Hungry," she says.

"Is that all you took?" Rays asks. "She's been waiting all day."

"The less I take the more often I can take it," I say, handing Kalika the flask. I am curious if she will notice the difference between my blood and Eric's. Actually, I wonder if she will drink it at all. But that doubt is soon dispelled. She wolves it down in a few gulps. The flask is thrust back into my hands.

"Hungry," Kalika says.

"I told you," Ray says. "You have to give her at least a pint."

I stare at Kalika, who stares back at me, and a curious sensation sweeps over me. There is a coldness in my daughter's eyes, but also a great expansive feeling. Few people in the West, who know anything of Vedic deities, understand the meaning of Kali or Kalika. To most she is simply a dark, bloodthirsty goddess. Yet that meaning is superficial, and I certainly would not have named my daughter after a monster with no redeeming virtues.

Actually, Kali *is* black, but this is because she represents space, the abyss, that which is before the creation, and that which will exist after. Her necklace of skulls symbolizes how she cares for souls after life, not just through one incarnation. Even the funeral pyre she sits on is representative of the many sins she burns to ash, when she is pleased. Kali is a destroyer, true, but she also destroys evil. Many of India's greatest saints worshipped her as the supreme being.

And they say she is easy to please—if one is careful.

Staring at my daughter, I am reminded of Krishna.

Yet Krishna had love as well as infinity.

Kalika has never been an affectionate child.

There is a bloodstain on her right cheek.

"Hungry, Mommy," she says softly.

Sighing, I take the flask and trudge back into the spare bedroom. Eric is upset to see me again so soon. Now this won't hurt a bit. I have to hit him again to get him to sit still, and I hate myself for the cruelty. I hate Krishna as well, for forcing me into this situation. But I know it is useless to hate God. It is like screaming at the night sky. The stars have no ears, and besides, they are too far away to hear. They just keep on shining, I must keep on living until death reaches my front door, or my own daughter comes for my blood in the dead of night. I have no doubt that, in a few days, she will be capable of killing me.

10

After boarding up Eric's room and ditching his car a safe distance away, I go for another drive, this one entirely aimless. It is dark now and the time of day suits my mood. Kalika thrust back her second empty eight-ounce glass of blood with the same numbing words: *Hungry, Mommy.* I shudder to think what her appetite will demand tomorrow. Will I have to collect a whole team of basketball players? Maybe I should drive down to the Forum and wait for the Lakers to start practice. They have some big boys who know how to shoot a ball.

But should they bleed for my daughter?

Should Eric?

Seymour has scored with many of his points, as always.

Midnight finds me at the beach where I buried Yaksha's body, or rather, where I sunk it. There was little of Yaksha left when I sent him to a watery grave, with his full blessings. Eddie Fender had done his usual number on my creator: stabbed him, torn him, dissected him, drained him. Good old Eddie, never one to take a joke well. But Yaksha hadn't minded the horrific treatment. Indeed, in the end, the most feared of all earth's ancient demons had found peace of mind through faith in Krishna. Staring at the dark waves, I think of how the passage of the many years does not necessarily bring devotion, how my own suffering has more often than not brought cynicism.

I have to wonder if that is why I keep suffering.

"What am I missing?" I ask the ocean. "Why do I have to go on like this?"

Yet now it is more important than ever that I continue. I am a mother; I have a responsibility to feed my daughter; but it is very possible my daughter is capable of destroying all mankind. No one knows, except perhaps Krishna, what weird alchemy of blood she possesses. Bowing my head in the direction of Yaksha's grave, I turn and leave the beach.

Another hour finds me at Paula's school, inside St. Andrews church. It's peculiar how many churches don't have posted hours, how their doors are always open. The light of the candles, as I step inside, fill me with warm feelings. Despite my obsession with Krishna, my respect for Jesus has never faded, even during the Middle Ages when the Catholic Church tried to burn me at the stake for witchcraft. Me, a witch? I'm a goddamn vampire. I almost told them that, but then, the Church was never one to enjoy a joke.

St. Andrews is comfortably stuffy. The smoke from the candles and incense fills my nostrils as I take a seat in the third pew and stare at the stained-glass windows, dark and sinister without the sun to give them color. A statue of Mother Mary stands nearby, dozens of glowing red dishes flickering at her feet. I have never lit a candle for the Madonna in the last two thousand years, but I have a strong urge to do so now. But I won't pray to her, I won't ask for her help. Her own son was crucified, so I don't think she is the best person to run to with my problems. Yet I feel close to her, and that is reason enough to show her respect. Plus I like candles. I like fire of all kinds.

I have just lit my candles when I hear steps off to my right.

"Alisa?"

I smile as I turn. "Paula. What are you doing here at this hour? Praying?"

She is happy to see me. As best as she can with her swollen belly, she gives me a hug. "No, I was working on the school's books. I couldn't sleep tonight. I only stopped in here because I saw a car parked out front. I thought it might be yours. Why are you here?"

I gesture to Mother Mary. "I'm making my confession."

"You need a priest for that."

I shake my head. "I don't think there's a priest anywhere who would be able to sit through a list of my sins."

"Nonsense. They hear all kinds of stuff. None of us is that unique. I think it all sounds the same to them after a while."

"For once I have to disagree with you. My confession would set a record for the most difficult penance assigned." I pause as a wave of nostalgia sweeps over me. "Actually, I knew a Catholic priest once. He used to listen to my confessions. I think that's what drove him mad."

Paula wonders if I am kidding. "What was his name?"

"Arturo. He was Italian. I met him in Florence, a long time ago. But that is another story. I'm happy to see you. How are you feeling?"

Paula beams. "Wonderful. If I didn't have such trouble sleeping, I wouldn't even know I was pregnant."

"Not to mention the basketball in your belly. Well, that's great, I'm happy for you." I glance at the main crucifix and lower my voice. "Very happy."

Paula touches my arm. "Something's the matter?"

I nod grimly, still staring at Jesus, wondering how it felt to hang on the cross with so much power available to him, but unable to show it. In that instant I feel a great kinship with Jesus. Seldom in five thousand years was I allowed to demonstrate my full power, and then, when I did, people died.

Also, I think of how Krishna was killed, cut down in the forest by a hunter's arrow, mistaken for a beast and shot in the heel, the only portion of his divine body that was vulnerable to physical attack. So the legend of Achilles was born, not in Greece, but in the deep forests of central India. It is impossible for me to look at Jesus and not think of Krishna. Honestly, all the religious dogma aside, I believe they were one and the same. So universal that they were everybody, and nobody at the same time. Like Kali, Mother Kalika.

Who is my daughter? What is she?

"Something is the matter," I say to Paula.

"What is it? Maybe I can help."

"No. Thanks, but no. No one can help me." I gesture to the empty pews. "Could I remain here a while? I have to think, to meditate. I think that will clear my mind, and then I will know what to do."

Paula kisses me on the cheek. "Stay as long as you want. I will lock the doors as I leave, but they will still open from the inside. You'll be safe in here."

I smile feebly. "Thank you. You are a true friend. Sometime, when things are less hectic, we must talk."

Paula stares deep into my eyes. "I look forward to that talk."

When she is gone, I curl up in one of the pews and close my eyes. I meditate best when I am unconscious, when I allow God to do most of the talking. Even though I am in a Catholic church, I pray Krishna will visit me in my dreams.

11

The scene is the same as it has always been. It can be no other way for it is constructed in eternity. It is only here that dialogue with the Almighty can take place.

I stand on a vast grassy plain with many gently sloping hills surrounding me. It is night, yet the sky is bright. A hundred blue stars blaze overhead. The air is warm and fragrant. In the distance a stream of people move slowly toward a large spaceship. The ship is violet; bright rays of light stab into the sky from it. I know that I am supposed to be on this ship. Yet, before I go to it, I have something to discuss with Lord Krishna.

He stands beside me on the plain, his gold flute in his right hand, a red lotus flower in his left. His dress, like mine, is simple—a long blue gown that reaches to the ground. But he wears a jewel around his neck—the brilliant Kaustubha gem, in which the destiny of every soul can be seen. He does not look at me but at the vast ship, and the stars beyond. He waits for me to speak, to answer him, but for some reason I can't remember what he last said. I only know that I am a special case. Because I do now know how to respond, I say what is most on my mind.

"When will I see you again, my Lord?"

He gestures to the wide plain, the stars overhead. "All this creation is an ocean, turbulent on the surface, silent in the depths. But like an ocean, the creatures in it are always searching for meaning in the creation, the ultimate element." He smiles to himself at the irony. "The fish searches for water in the ocean. He has heard so much about it. But he never finds it, and that is because he searches too hard." He pauses. "I am everywhere in the creation. There is nowhere that I am not. Why do you speak to me of separation?"

"Because, my Lord, I fear I will forget you when I enter into the creation."

He shrugs, he has no worries. "That is to be expected. You learn by forgetting what you once knew. Then, when you remember, it is that much sweeter."

"When will you come to earth?"

"When I am least expected."

"Will I see you, my Lord?"

"Yes, twice. At the beginning of Kali Yuga and then at the end of the age."

"Will I recognize you?"

"Not at first, not with the mind. But inside you will know me."

"How will I know you?"

He looks at me then, and his eyes are a wonder, windows into the cosmos. Time loses all meaning. It is as if the whole universe turns while I stare at him. I see thousands of people, millions of stars, so much life striving for small joys, so many illusions ending in shattering bitterness. Yet in the end it all turns to red, then to black, as the blood of the people runs cold and the fires of Kali burn the galaxies to ash. Still, none of this disturbs the eternal Lord for he never blinks, even though the sheer magnitude of the vision forces me to turn away trembling. He has stolen my very breath.

"Sri Krishna," I pray, overwhelmed, "take my soul now. Don't send me out. I surrender everything to you. I can't bear to forget you even for a moment."

He smiles. "I will tell you a story. This same story will be told by a simple man named Jesus, in the middle of Kali Yuga. Few people will recognize this Jesus with their minds, but some will know him inside." Krishna pauses before he begins.

"There is a man named Homa, who is a good person but not a perfect soul. He is a friend of Jesus and one day Jesus asks him to go to the village to buy some food for a large meal Jesus wants to give for some elders of the nearby village. Jesus says to the man, 'Take these ten coins and buy twelve loafs of bread, five jugs of wine, four fish, and one bag of a grain. Load it all on my donkey, and when you are done bring it here. I will be waiting for you.'

"At this Homa is confused, as well as excited with

greed. He can see Jesus does not understand the value of the coins because he knows he can get all the things Jesus has requested for only five coins. Yet Homa also knows Jesus will need twice as much as he has asked for in order to feed all the people who are expected. Still, Homa does not plan on spending all ten coins. He says to himself, 'I will buy what I have been told to buy, and I will pocket the rest of the coins.'

"So Homa takes the donkey to town, and sets about purchasing the food. At the bakery he buys twelve loafs of bread, but as he places them on the donkey, when he is not looking, they change to twenty-four loafs. Next, Homa gets the five jugs of wine and the four fish. But like before, when he is not looking, the five jugs turns to ten, and the four fish turn to eight. Finally, Homa obtains the bag of grain, but then, on the way back, he sees that he actually has two bags, and that everything else has doubled as well. He is astounded and feels to see if the five coins are still in his pocket.

"Jesus is waiting for him when he arrives and greets him with a kind smile. The smile of Jesus is a wonderful thing. Mankind's history will portray Jesus as filled with sorrow, but the love and joy that flow toward Homa when Jesus looks at him is all-consuming. Still, Homa is worried about seeing Jesus, even though Jesus has only kind words for him.

"Jesus says, 'Welcome back, Homa, you have brought everything we need for a great feast. Thank you.'

"But in shame Homa lowers his head and takes the five coins and places them at Jesus' feet. 'Don't thank me, Master, for I thought to cheat you. I knew you needed more than you asked for, but I was going to keep these extra coins for myself. It is only by some strange magic that all this food is here. I bought only half this.' At that he kisses Jesus' feet. 'I am unworthy to be called your friend, or even your servant.'

"But Jesus lifts him up, and says, 'No, Homa, you have done well because you have done my bidding. That is all you have to do. I ask nothing more of anyone.' "

Krishna pauses and stares up at the sky. "Did you enjoy this story?"

"Yes, my Lord. But I do not know if I understand it, or how it relates to me."

"This man, Homa, he is like every man. He is good-hearted but he has his flaws. Yet he is perfect in the eyes of Jesus because he has done what Jesus asks. You see, Sita, God does not expect you to give him all that you have. He understands the ways of the world, that it requires effort to deal with them. God only asks that you grant him half of what you possess, and then God will make up the other half. That is why the food multiplied. That is the miracle of this tale." Krishna pauses. "This story will be a part of the Gospel of Jesus, but too soon it will be removed from the holy book by those who want the peasant class to give everything to the Church, who do not understand the compassion of Jesus for those who struggle in the world." Krishna pauses again and smiles at me, that bewitching smile that steals even the hearts of the gods. "You don't need to surrender *everything* to me. Keep your head and I will take your heart. You will need your head to deal with Kali Yuga, particularly the end of the age."

"What will happen at the end, my Lord?"

Krishna laughs and raises his flute to his lips. "You will not enjoy the tale if you know the end of the tale. Enough questions, Sita, now listen to my song. It dispels all illusions, all suffering. When you feel lost, remember it, remember me, and you see the things you desire most are the very things that bring you the greatest sorrow. My song is eternal, it can be heard at all times in all places."

"But—"

"Listen, Sita. Listen in silence."

Krishna starts to play. But as he does, a sudden wind comes up on the plain and the notes of his melody are drowned out. The dust rises and I am blinded, and I can't see Krishna anymore. The light of the stars fades and everything turns black.

Yet in this blackness an even darker shadow fills the sky, and I know I see Kali, who is without color and who destroys all at the end of time. Sinners as well as saints, devils as well as angels, humans as well as vampires. And I know it is Kali who will eventually destroy me.

12

Over the next three days Kalika grows to the approximate age of five, while Eric ages ten years. During this time she reads greedily and masters English, as well as many subtleties of conversation and social convention. I have tested her—her IQ appears off the charts. Her beauty flourishes as well. Her long dark hair is like a shawl of black silk, her face a fine sculpture of hidden mysteries. Even her voice is magic, filled with haunting rhythms. When she speaks, it is hard not to listen, to agree with her, to forget everything else. But it is seldom Kalika does speak, and what runs through her mind—besides her hunger for blood—I have no idea.

It is in the middle of night when my daughter wakes me in my bed. She does this by gently stroking my hair. I am forced to wake to confusion.

"I can't wait," she says. "I need more."

I shake my head. "He can't take it. You're going to have to wait till later in the day. I have to get you another."

Kalika is gently persistent. "I can do it if you don't want to. I know how."

I frown. "Have you been watching me?" Naturally, I have not let Eric see where his blood is going. Somehow I doubt it would lift his spirits.

"Yes," Kalika says. "I watch you."

I sit up. "Has he seen you?"

"No." She pauses and glances at Ray, who continues to sleep. "He hasn't seen either of us."

"You are not listening to me. This boy can give no more blood. Already his heartbeat is erratic. In a few hours, when it is light, I will go out and find another supply. Until then you will have to be patient."

Kalika stares at me with her dark blue eyes. Perhaps it is my imagination, but I catch a glimmer of red in their depths. She smiles slightly, showing her front teeth.

"I have been patient, Mother." That is her new name for me. "I will just take a little of his blood, and then we can go for another supply. We can go in a few minutes."

I snort. "You're not going with me. You're a little girl."

Kalika is unmoved. "I will come with you. You will need me."

I pause. "Do you know that for sure?"

"Yes."

"I don't believe you."

Kalika loses her smile. "I won't lie to you, Mother, if you don't lie to me."

"Don't give me orders. You are to do what I say at all times. Is that clear?"

She nods. "As long as you don't lie to me." She adds, as if it were related, "How is Paula doing?"

Her question confuses me. Kalika has never met Paula. How would I explain that I have given birth to a child and that she has grown to five years of age, all in a month? Of course, I have talked about Paula with Ray. Perhaps Kalika was listening.

"Why do you ask?" I say.

Kalika glances at Ray. "I am curious about her. She means a lot to you."

"She's my friend. She's doing fine. One day you will meet her."

"Do you promise?"

I hesitate. "We'll see." I throw off the covers and put my feet on the floor. "We can go out now, if you insist. But we're not disturbing Eric anymore."

Kalika puts a hand on my leg. It is still a small hand but I have to wonder if I would be able to stand if she didn't want me to. I doubt it, and do not try to brush her fingers away.

It is a terrible thing to be afraid of one's own daughter.

"I will take only a little of his blood," she repeats.

"How much?"

"Eight ounces."

"That is not a little, not for him. He is weak, don't you care?"

Kalika is thoughtful. When she gets that way, she stares at the ground. I have no idea what she looks for. Her eyes close halfway, and her breathing seems to halt. The overall effect is disturbing. Finally she looks up.

"I care," she says. "But not in the way you mean."

I am curious. She is still an enigma to me. "What do you mean?"

She shakes her head. "I cannot explain, Mother."

Kalika leaves me to get dressed. Knocking lightly on Eric's door, I step in his room. I have not been able to untie him as I had hoped. As his strength has failed, his behavior has become more desperate. He thinks only of escape, or of his own impending death. I wish I could release him. An unhappy bundle of nerves stuffed in a stale corner, he twitches as I step into the room.

"No," he moans. "I can't."

I kneel by his side. "I need just a little. Less than last time."

He weeps. "Why?"

"You know I can't tell you why. But it will be over soon, Eric, I promise. I'm going out right now to—to get someone else."

He shakes his head sadly as he stares up at the ceiling. "I'm not stupid. You're never going to let me go. You're going to keep me here till I die."

"No."

He speaks with passion. "Yes. You're evil. You're a vampire. You have to kill me to keep your evil ways secret."

His words hurt. "I'm not a vampire. I don't take this blood for myself."

He is not listening. He continues to sob but grows more animated. "You're some monster from another planet. You're going to rip me open and eat my guts. You're going to have a glass of wine and have my guts all over your face, dripping on your clothes, on the floor . . ." He raises his voice. "You're going to eat me alive!"

"Shh."

"You're an alien monster!"

"Eric!"

"Help! The monster's got me! The aliens are coming!"

I am forced to strike him hard in the face to shut him up. My reflexes are still excellent, my martial art skills sharp. I believe I break his nose. Yet he continues to moan softly as I tighten the tourniquet. After I have drained away eight ounces—I know Kalika will count them—he dozes, probably out of sheer loss of blood. I kiss the top of his head before I leave the room.

"You will go home, Eric," I whisper. "I am not a monster."

While Kalika has her breakfast, I dress in my bedroom, in black leather pants, a tight leather coat. Ray sits up in bed. I do not need to turn to feel his eyes on me.

"Are you going out?" he asks.

"Yes. You know why."

"Yes. You've waited too long anyway."

"It's not an enjoyable task, you know, finding people to kill."

"Eric's still alive."

"Barely."

"Find someone you don't like. A criminal, a rapist—you used to specialize in them if I remember correctly."

I turn on him. "I may not be able to handle a criminal or rapist nowadays, or does that concern you, my love?"

He shrugs. "Take your pistol. It has a silencer on it. Just get someone you're not going to go to pieces over every time you have to take blood."

I speak with thinly disguised bitterness. "You didn't answer my question, my love. But I suppose that is answer enough. You know I enjoy this little family we have here. A gorgeous daughter who is a medical and historical first, and a supposedly loving boyfriend who has forgotten what the words *friend* and *love* mean. I mean, you've got to admit, five thousand years of intense experience has really helped me create the perfect domestic environment. Wouldn't you agree?"

He is unimpressed by my outburst. "You create

what you want. You always have. If you don't like it, you can always leave."

I snort. "Leave you with Kalika! She would starve in a day."

"I doubt that Kalika will need either of us soon. She's not a normal child, you know." He adds, "Not like Paula's child will be."

I stop. "Why did you say that?"

He ignores me. "When is her baby due exactly? Soon?"

I frown. Why were they both dropping remarks about Paula? "She's not having a baby anymore," I say carefully. "She lost it."

He waves his hand. "Yeah, right, she got kicked by a donkey."

A donkey, I think. "Yeah, that is right." I turn away. "Seymour was right about you."

Ray is instantly alert. "You spoke to him. When did you speak to him?"

I reach for my black boots. "None of your business."

"What did he say about me?"

I glare at him. "He said that Eddie Fender's blood has warped your mind. He told me not to trust you, which was probably good advice."

Eric relaxes. "Good old Seymour. Did you invite him down for a pleasant evening of food and conversation?"

I have my boots on and stalk out the door. "He is not interested in our problems," I lie. "He has better things to do with his time."

But Ray's final remark makes me pause outside the door.

"I hope you didn't tell him about Kalika. I really hope you didn't."

I glance over my shoulder. "Of course not. He would never have believed me if I had."

Ray just nods and smiles.

13 ~

Kalika drives with me to a club in Hollywood. It is one in the morning but the place is still hopping. What I'm supposed to do with my daughter, I'm not sure. It is she who suggests she hide under a blanket in the backseat until I bring out whoever it is who is to be our next barrel of blood. As she crawls under the blanket, she peers up at me with her serious dark blue eyes.

"You'll be warm enough?" I ask.

"I am never cold," she says.

"If you want, you can sleep. Just don't make any noise when I return to the car. I'll take care of everything." I glance at the crowded parking lot. "But I won't be able to knock him out here."

"Take him to a secluded place," Kalika says. "I will help you."

"I told you, I don't want your help."

Kalika does the unexpected then. She reaches up and kisses me on the lips. "Be careful, Mother. You are not who you used to be."

Her kiss warms me, her words give me a chill. "You know what I used to be?"

"Yes. He told me."

"Ray?"

"Yes."

"How come you never call him Father?"

"You call him Ray. I call him Ray."

"But he calls me Sita."

"Do you want me to call you Sita?"

"No, it doesn't matter." I pause. "Do you like Ray?"

She shrugs. "How I feel—I can't explain to you at this time."

"Why not?"

"You are not ready to hear."

"When will I be ready to hear?"

"Soon."

"You know this?"

She pulls the blanket over her head. "I know many things, Mother."

The music is loud as I enter the club, the strobe lights flashing, unnatural thunder and psychedelic solar flares to match the scrambled brains of the alcohol-saturated clientele. I am, of course, a superb dancer, even without my vampire strength. Without looking around, I leap onto the dance floor and wait for my daughter's next meal to come to me. Guilt makes me less discriminating. Let destiny decide who is to suffer, I will not.

A man about thirty, with an expensive sports coat and a thin black mustache joins me within a few minutes. His speech is educated; he could be an Ivy League graduate, a young lawyer with something profitable on the side. His watch is a Rolex, his single gold earring studded with a carat diamond. He is not handsome but his face is likable. He speaks smoothly.

"Mind if I butt in?" he asks.

I smile, whirling, my hair in my eyes. "There's no one to butt out."

He chuckles. "Hey, you're a real dancer."

"You're not bad yourself. What's your name?"

"Billy. You?"

"Cynthia. But you can call me Cindy."

He grins, he's having a good time. "I'll call you whatever you want."

After twenty minutes on the floor, he buys me a couple of drinks. We catch our breath over them at the bar. I was right, he's a lawyer but he insists he's an honest one.

"I don't represent shmucks and I don't fudge my billing hours," he says proudly, sipping his Bloody Mary, my drink of choice when I am on the prowl. I am already on my second. The alcohol soothes my nerves, although I don't suppose it sharpens my reflexes. At my waist, above my butt and beneath my leather jacket, I carry my pistol and silencer. But I know I won't need it on Billy. He will go the way of

Eric, to endless misery. Guilt hangs over my head but I keep it away with a stiff umbrella of denial.

"What firm are you with?" I ask.

"Gibson and Pratch. They're in Century City. I live in the valley. The traffic's hell coming over the San Diego Freeway in the morning. What do you do?"

"I'm a music teacher," I say.

"Cool. What instrument do you play?"

"Piano, some violin."

"Wow, that's incredible. I have an expensive piano that was left to me by my rich uncle. I've always meant to take lessons, but never got around to it." He pauses and then has a brilliant idea. God inspires it. I know what it is; he hasn't been able to take his eyes off my body. "Hey, will you play me something on my piano?"

I laugh and look around. "Did you bring it with you?"

"No, at my place. It doesn't take long to get there at this time of night."

I hesitate. "Like you say, Billy, it's late. I have to get up in the morning."

"Nah! You're a teacher. You call your students and tell them when you want to see them. Really, we can go in my car. I've got a brand-new Jag."

I'm impressed. "I love Jags." I glance uneasily at my watch, playing the role to the hilt. "OK, but I'm going to have to follow you there. That way I can head straight back to my place after your song."

Billy is pleased as he sets down his drink. "I'll drive slowly. I won't lose you."

Kalika is asleep when I return to the car. Her soft

rhythmic breathing follows me as I steam onto the freeway and chase Billy's Jag into the valley. He has lied to me—he drives like a maniac.

My plan is simple. I will knock him out the second we get inside, then load him into my trunk. He looks like he's been drinking all night, an easy mark. He won't even know what hit him.

Kalika is still asleep when we reach Billy's place.

I leave my gun in the glove compartment.

Billy's house is modest, considering his new car. The driveway is cracked, the landscaping neglected. He lives in a cul-de-sac. His car disappears into the automatic garage as I park in the street. A moment later he is on the front porch, waving to me. Making sure Kalika is resting comfortably, I get out and walk toward Billy, my boots clicking on the asphalt and concrete. Billy thinks he's in for a night of sex and more sex. His grin as he greets me belongs to a sixteen-year-old. I'm not surprised when he kisses me the moment we're inside with the door closed. His mouth is sweet with the taste of alcohol, his groping hands moist with the thrill of seduction. He presses me against the wall and I have to turn my head to catch my breath.

"Hold on a second, Billy," I protest. "You haven't even shown me the house. And where's your piano?"

He stares at me with a gleam in his eye. "I don't have a piano."

"What do you mean. You said your uncle . . ."

"I don't have an uncle," he interrupts.

Right then I smell it. The odor is faint, probably something most young women would miss, but I have had extensive experience with this smell. I don't need supernatural nostrils to identify it. Somewhere in Billy's house, perhaps buried beneath his bed, perhaps cemented into his bathroom floor, is one or more dead bodies. My best estimate as I look deeper into his manic eyes is that it is more than one. I curse myself for being such a fool, for being caught off guard. Certainly as a vampire I would have heard his lies a mile away.

Careful, I let none of my insights show on my face.

"That's all right, Billy," I say. "I don't know how to play piano anyway."

He is dizzy with pleasure. "You lied to me?"

"We lied to each other."

There is a single metal click. The sound is very specific, the snap of a switchblade. His right arm begins to slash upward. He is close to me, though, perhaps too close. Giving him a nudge in the chest, I yank my right knee up as hard as I can, catching him clean in the groin. But Billy must have balls of steel. My blow stuns him but he doesn't double up in agony. His switchblade continues its terrifying course toward my throat. Only by twisting to the side at the last second do I manage to avoid having my jugular severed. But even though I momentarily break free, the blade catches the tip of my left shoulder and slices through my leather jacket. The knife is incredibly sharp; it opens a four-inch gash in my tender flesh. Blood spurts from my body as I stagger into the center of the living room.

How I long for my pistol right then.

Billy limps toward me, holding his bloody knife in

his right hand, his bruised balls in his left. He grins again but he is no longer a happy-go-lucky serial killer.

"You are a spunky little bitch," he says.

I grab a vase of flowers and cock it back in my right hand. "Stop! I'll scream if you don't."

He laughs. "My nearest neighbors are all old and hard of hearing. This house is completely soundproof. Scream all you want, Cindy."

"My name's not Cindy. Your's isn't Billy."

He is surprised. "Who are you then?"

"Why should I tell you?"

"Because I want to know before you die."

I harden my voice. "I am Sita, of the ancient past. I am older than I look and I have dealt with scum like you before. It is you who will die this night, and I don't care what your name is."

He charges, and he moves fast for a nonvampire. The vase, of course, I throw at him merely to upset his balance. But he seems to know that ahead of time; he ducks and prepares for my real blow. I am already in the air, however, lashing out with my right foot, the heel of my boot, aiming for the sensitive spot on his jaw that professional boxers covet. One hard punch will put him out cold.

Unfortunately my human muscles fail me once again. I am short on the reach. As a result my devastating kick barely contacts his jaw. The blow backs him up, cuts him even, but it by no means puts him down. Wiping at his face, he has hatred in his eyes.

"Where did you learn this stuff?" he demands.

"Through a correspondance course," I snap as I begin to circle. Now I have lost the element of surprise. He watches my feet as he stalks me with his knife. Someone has trained him as well, I see. He does not lunge carelessly, but plots his strikes. One such swipe of his knife slashes open the back of my right hand. The pain is electric, burning, my blood is everywhere. Still, I maintain my balanced stance, circling, searching for an opening. He is skilled at defense; however, he never stops moving his arms. I know I can't let him catch my leg. He would probably saw off my foot, and make me watch.

Then he makes a mistake. Going for my eyes, he subtly telegraphs his intention. My initial reaction is simple—I duck. Then I leap up just after the knife swishes over my head and sweep his lower legs with my left foot. The move is kung fu, very old and effective. Billy, or whoever the hell he is, topples to the floor. I am on him in an instant. When he tries to rise, I kick him in the face, then again in the chest. He smashes into his coffee table and his knife bounces on the blood-stained carpet and I kick it away. Lying on his back, breathing hard, he stares at me in amazement. Standing over him, I feel the old satisfaction of triumph. I step on his left wrist and pin his arm to the floor.

"I actually can play the piano," I say. "If you had an instrument here, I would play Mozart's *Requiem* for the dead after I stuff you in a closet."

He still has a weird gleam in his eye. "Is your name really Sita?"

"Yes."

"How old are you? You're older than you look, huh?"

"Yes. How old are you and how do you want to die?"

He grins. "I'm not going to die."

"No?"

"No." And with that, before I can react, he pulls out a snub-nose silver revolver and points it at my head. "Not tonight, Sita."

Once again I am furious at myself, for not taking him out immediately when he was helpless. I know what my problem is. I am used to playing with my victims, a luxury I can no longer afford now that I am mortal. There is no way I can dodge the bullet he can send hurtling into my brain. It is his game now. Taking my foot off his wrist, I back up a couple of steps. He gets up slowly and guards me carefully. He is not one to repeat a mistake, as the odor in his house testifies.

"How many girls have you cut up here?" I ask.

"Twelve. The youngest was five." He grins. "You're going to be lucky number thirteen."

"Thirteen is traditionally an unlucky number," I remind him.

He gestures with his gun. "On your knees. Keep your hands on top of your head. No sudden moves."

I do as he says. Like I have a lot of choice. The blood from my hand wound drips into my hair and over my face. Like those of a full-fledged vampire, my tears are once again dark red. My situation is clearly desperate, and I cannot think of a clear course of action. He ties my wrists behind my back with nylon cord. Although I can work my way out of any knot, even with my current strength, he complicates my dilemma by redoing the knots several times over. When he is finished he crouches in front of me and takes out his switchblade. He plays with my hair with the tip of the blade, with my eyes even, letting the silver razor brush the surface of the whites. I won't be surprised if he gouges one of my eyes out and eats it.

"You're so beautiful," he says.

"Thank you."

"All my girls have been beautiful. I don't *carve* them unless they are."

I have to restrain myself from spitting in his face. "Why do you *carve* them?"

"To give them more dimension. I enjoy it."

"Obviously."

He leans close, his breath on my face, his knife now inside my right nostril. "You know, I never met a girl like you. Not only can you fight, you are totally fearless."

I smile sweetly. "Yeah, I could be your partner. Why don't you untie me and we can talk about it?"

He laughs. "See! That's exactly what I mean. You make jokes in the face of death." He slides the knife a little farther up my nose and loses his smile. A typical serial killer, moody as hell. "But some of your jokes aren't that funny. Some of them annoy me. I don't like to annoyed."

I swallow thickly. "I can understand that."

He pokes the inside of my nose and a narrow line of blood pours over my mouth and down my throat. His eyes are inches from mine, his mouth almost close enough to lick my blood. I am afraid he will do that next, and not like the taste. It hurts to have a switchblade up my right nostril. Still, I cannot think of a way out of my situation. Yet I find I am more concerned about Kalika, asleep in the car, than I am about myself. Truly I am a good mother. It was only my love for my daughter that brought me into this evil place. Krishna will understand.

I feel I will be seeing him soon.

"You know what I don't like about you?" he asks. "It's your cockiness. I had a cocky girlfriend in high school once. Her name was Sally and she was so sure of herself." He pauses. "Until she lost her nose and her lips. A girl with only half a face is never a smart mouth."

I wisely keep my mouth shut.

There is a knock at the front door.

Billy pulls the knife higher, still inside my nose, forcing my head back. "Don't make a sound," he whispers. "There is dying all at once and there is dying piece by piece. Believe me, I can take a week to kill you if you try to get their attention."

My eyelashes flash up and down. Yes, I understand and agree.

I know who is at the door. The person knocks again.

Billy is sweating. Clearly he fears some noise has escaped his soundproof spider's lair and that a neighbor has called the police. All he can do is wait and worry. But he is not kept in suspense long. The door slowly opens and a beautiful five-year-old girl with stunning dark hair and large black-blue eyes pokes her head inside.

"Mother," Kalika says. "Are you OK?"

Billy is astounded and immensely relieved. He lowers his switchblade. "Is that your daughter?" he asks.

"Yes."

"What is she doing here?"

"She came with me. She was sleeping in the car."

"Well, I'll be goddamned. I didn't know you had a daughter."

"There are a few things about me you don't know." I glance at Kalika, wondering what I should do: be a good mother, warn her to get away, or remain silent and try to get out of this hell hole alive. Honestly, I don't know how quick Kalika is, exactly how strong she is. But a vampire her size and her age could take Billy. I speak carefully, "I am not OK, darling."

"I told you," she replies.

Billy withdraws his knife and stands in front of me. He is bleeding as well, and he has plenty of my blood on him. He holds his messy knife in his right hand and he has his shiny revolver tucked in his belt. Plus the light in his eyes is radioactive. He looks as trustworthy as Jack the Ripper on a PCP high. Yet he gestures to Kalika to come closer, as if he were Santa Claus anxious to hear her wish list.

"Come here, darling," he says in a sweet voice.

And she comes, slowly, observing every blessed detail: the composition of the floor, how Billy stands, the height of the ceiling, the arrangement of the furniture—moving precisely the way an experienced vampire would move while closing in for the kill. Her arms hang loose by her sides, her legs slightly apart, well-balanced, and she is up on her toes so that she can move either way fast. Billy senses there is something odd about her. When she is ten feet from him, he drops his smile. For my apart, I watch in wonder and terror. Only then do I realize the full extent of my love for my daughter. I would rather die a dozen times over than have anything happen to her.

"What's your name, sweetie?" Billy asks when she stops directly in front of him. His voice is uneasy, perhaps as a result of the power of her stare, which is now locked on his face. Kalika tilts her head slightly to one side, ignoring me for the moment.

"Kalika," she says.

He frowns. "What kind of name is that, child?"

"It's a Vedic name. It's who I am."

"What does it mean?" he asks.

"It has many meanings. Most of them are secret." She finally gestures to me. "You've hurt my mother. She's bleeding."

Billy gives an exaggerated sigh. "I know that Kalika, and I'm sorry. But it was your mother who hurt me first. I only hurt her back to defend myself."

Kalika doesn't blink. "You are lying. You are not a good man. But your blood is good. I will drink it in a moment." She pauses. "You can put your knife and your gun down now. You will not need them."

Billy is having a night of amazement. His face breaks into a wolfish grin and he looks down at me. "What kind of nonsense have you been teaching this child, Sita?"

I shrug. "She watches too much TV."

Billy snorts. "God, I can't believe this family." He takes a step toward my daughter, his knife still in his right hand. "Come here, girl. I'm putting you in the other room. I have business with your mother that can't wait. But I'll let you out in a little while, if you behave yourself." Billy holds out his free hand. "Come, give me your hand."

Kalika innocently reaches up and takes his hand. She even allows his fingers to close around her tiny digits. But then, in a move too swift for human eyes to properly follow, she grabs his other hand, twists his wrist at an impossible angle, and rams the knife into his stomach. Literally the blade is sunk up to the hilt. An expression of surprise and grief swallows Billy's face as he stares down at what she has done to him. Slowly, as if in a dream, he lets go of the knife. It is obvious his right wrist is broken. Blood gushes over his pants and Kalika stares at it with her first sign of pleasure.

"I am hungry," she says.

Billy gasps for air but finally he is getting the idea that he is in mortal danger, that he might be, in fact, already screwed. Summoning his failing strength, he makes a swipe for Kalika's head. But she is not standing where she was an instant before, and he misses. She is her mother's daughter. Twice she kicks with her right foot, with her shiny black shoes that I bought for her at the mall, and the cartilage in both his joints explodes. Falling to his shattered knees, he lets out a pitiful scream.

"How can you do this to me?" he cries.

Kalika steps over and grabs him by his hair and pulls his head back, exposing his throat. The calm on her face is eerie even for me to see.

"If you understood the full meaning of my name," she says, "you would have no need to ask."

Billy dies piece by piece, drop by drop.

Kalika satisfies herself before she releases me.

Even I, Sita the Damned, cannot bear to watch.

14

The following week Kalika attains full maturity, approximately twenty years of age, about the same age I was when I was changed into a vampire. At this point her growth seems to halt. I am not surprised. It is a fact that a human being is at his or her greatest strength, mentally and physically, just out of his or her teens. Certainly Kalika is very powerful, but how powerful I'm not sure. Except for the incident with Billy, she never demonstrates her abilities in front of me. One thing is sure, though—she no longer needs me to bring her lunch. Now she leaves the house for long stretches of time—on foot and at night. When she returns, I don't ask where she's been or who she's been with. I don't want to know.

Of course that's a lie. I scrutinize the papers each day for reports of unexplained murders. Yet I find none, and it makes me wonder.

The police have yet to find Billy—what is left of him. I know it is only a matter of time. I hope they will uncover his victims as well.

My hand and shoulder are still bandaged. I did not allow myself the luxury of a doctor and hospital, but I did manage to sew myself up fairly well. Still, I know I will be scarred for life.

The change in my daughter's eating habits means that I no longer need to keep Eric locked in the spare bedroom. Unfortunately, I can't figure out a way to let him go and keep him from running straight to the police. Simply moving to another city, or even another state, is not a solution. Well, it would probably help, but I don't want to move, not until Paula has her baby. Kalika and Ray don't want to move either. They have stated their opinion many times.

So I keep Eric locked up, but have stopped taking his blood. It had been my hope that this would cheer him up, and he'd be able to gain back his strength. But Eric is now deep in the throes of depression and won't eat a bite.

"Come on, Eric," I say as I offer him a hamburger and fries. "This is a McDonald's Big Mac and their golden delicious french fries, large size. I've even brought you a vanilla shake." I touch his head as he refuses to even look at me. He has lost over thirty pounds since meeting me, and his skin is a pasty yellow. There are black circles under his eyes, from his grief, and from the times I hit him. His nose is still broken; he has trouble breathing, especially tied up as he is. I add gently, "You've got to eat something. You're just wasting away in here."

"Then why don't you let me go like you promised?" he asks quietly. "I'm sick—you know I'm really sick."

"I am going to let you go. Just as soon as I figure out the logistics of the release. You understand I have to worry about you talking to the police. I have to be long gone from this place before you are freed."

"I won't talk to the police. I just want to go home."

"I know you do. It won't be long now." I push the hamburger his way. "Have a bite, just for me, and I'll have some of your fries. We can pretend we're in that coffee shop you took me to on our first date."

That is probably not the best thing to say. He begins to sob again. "I thought you were a nice girl. I just wanted to talk to you. I didn't know you would hurt me and take all my blood."

"But I stopped taking your blood. Things are looking up. Soon you'll see your mom and dad. And they'll be so excited to see you. Just think of that, Eric, and try to keep a positive attitude. Imagine what an incredible homecoming you're going to have. You'll be interviewed by every TV station in the country. You can even make your story more exciting than it really was. You can say how a whole horde of vampires tortured you night and day and used your blood for satanic rituals. The media will love that—they're really into the devil. You'll be a celebrity, a hero, and after that you'll probably get lots of dates. The girls will come to you. Heroes are sexy. You won't have to go looking for girls in the park."

My pep talk is wasted on him. He stares at me with bloodshot eyes and sniffles. "Even if you wanted to let me go, she'd never let you."

I pause. "Who's she?"

"The one you've been giving my blood to."

"I don't know what you're talking about."

"I've seen her. You serve her and you don't know it, but I know she's not human. I've seen her *eyes,* the red fire deep inside. She drinks human blood and she's evil." He nods like a man who's been granted a vision by God and won't be convinced otherwise. "After she kills me and eats my guts, she's going to kill you and eat your brains."

Well, I don't know what to say to that.

Placing the hamburger in his lap, I leave the room.

Ray is sitting in the living room. Kalika is in the backyard, sitting in the full lotus and meditating with her eyes closed in the bright sun, wearing a one-piece black bathing suit. She sits on a white towel in the center of the lawn and doesn't move a fraction of an inch, or even seem to breathe. This is a new habit of hers, but I am afraid to ask what she mediates on. Perhaps her own name, or the secret forms of it. They are reputed to be powerful mantras.

Ray looks up at me. "Is he eating?"

"No."

"What are we going to do with him?"

I sit on the couch across from Ray. "I don't know. Let him go."

"We can't let him go. Not now."

"Then we'll let him go later," I say.

Ray shakes his head. "I think that's a bad idea. It

will require us to cover our tracks. He'll just give the authorities information we don't want them to have. Think about it a minute before you dismiss it. You said yourself that the government might still be searching for you. What are they going to think when they hear the story of a young man who was held captive by a beautiful blond woman who systematically drained his blood? They'll put two and two together, and they'll start a manhunt for you unlike anything that's been seen in this country. Remember, they still want that vampire blood."

I speak in a flat voice. "What is it you want me to think about?"

Ray hesitates. "Just getting rid of the problem."

"You mean kill Eric and bury him in the backyard?"

"I don't think we should bury him there. But, yes, I don't see how we can let him go and expect to remain free ourselves."

I smile as I stare at him. It is one of those smiles a salesperson gives to a customer. "You know, something just occured to me."

"What?"

"I don't know who you are. Oh, you look like Ray. You talk like him and you even have his memories. But I honestly don't know who you are."

"Sita, be serious. You have to face reality."

"That's exactly what I'm doing. The Ray I met and loved would never talk about killing an innocent young man. No matter what the consequences to himself. The idea would never even enter his mind. And one more thing, I've been watching our daughter the last few days and I swear she doesn't look a bit like you. You don't share a single feature. How can that be?"

Ray snorts. "You're the one who should be able to answer that question. You're the one who got pregnant."

"I wish I could answer it. I believe if I could, many other questions would be answered as well."

"Such as?"

I lose my smile. "I don't know how much I should tell you. I don't trust you, and I'm not going to kill Eric. We'll leave here before it comes to that. I don't care if he does set the government on my tail."

"You will not leave here until Paula has her baby."

"Paula's baby is not the topic of this conversation. Also, I notice you're not responding to my accusations. You're not even trying to defend yourself."

"They're so ridiculous. What can I say?" He glances down the hall. "Eric has to die, and the sooner the better."

"Have you shared this with Kalika?"

"Yes."

"Does she agree with you?"

Ray is evasive. "She didn't say one way or the other."

"She never says much." I straighten up and point a finger at Ray. "But let's make one thing perfectly clear. If you so much as harm a single hair on Eric's head, you'll regret it."

Ray is amused. "You're not a vampire anymore. You have nothing to back up your threats.

I'm not given a chance to respond. By chance, if

anything is chance, a police car pulls into our driveway at that moment. The two officers are almost to the door when I remember that I have not replaced Eric's gag. I've been letting him be without it for the last few days. He knows the penalty for crying out.

Yet if he hears the police in the house, what will he do?

Ray runs into the back room, not into Eric's. I answer the door. A blond-haired cop and a dark-haired one. The handsome black one holds a picture of Eric in his hand. Wonderful.

"Hello," he says. "I'm Officer Williams and this is my partner, Officer Kent. We're canvassing the neighborhood for information concerning the whereabouts of this young man. His name is Eric Hawkins. He vanished close to three weeks ago." He pauses. "May we come in?"

"Sure." I open the door wider. As they step inside, I ask, "Was this guy from around here? Excuse me, please, have a seat."

Kent and Williams settle themselves on my couch. Williams does the talking. He is the leader of the two—his eyes are everywhere, searching for clues. Well-muscled Kent sits content like a comfortable jock after a hard game. I plop down across from them.

"Actually, Eric lives some distance from here," Williams says. "But we have a report from one of your neighbors that a guy who fit his description was seen entering your house. Also, this same neighbor believes she saw Eric's car parked out in front of your house on the day he disappeared."

"So you're not just canvassing the neighborhood.

You've come here specifically to see me?" I gesture to Eric's picture. "I've never seen this guy in my life."

Williams is grave. "We also have a description from two guys that Eric was playing basketball with on the day he disappeared. They say he left Scott Park in the company of a young woman who matches your description."

I raise my hand, palm out. "Hold on! You do not have *my* description. I don't even know where Scott Park is. What exactly did these guys say?"

Williams consults notes jotted on a piece of folded paper. "That he left the park in the company of a beautiful blond girl approximately eighteen to twenty-one. Her hair was long, like yours."

I'm not impressed. "There are literally tens of thousands of cute blond girls with long hair in Southern California."

"That is true ma'am," Williams says. "You're just a lead we're checking out." He pauses. "Did you have a guest with a blue Honda Civic park in your driveway three weeks ago?"

"I can't remember. Lots of friends drop by. They have all kinds of cars."

"Do you have a friend who looks like Eric?" Williams asks. "Someone your neighbor might have mistakenly identified as Eric."

I shrug. "I have a couple of friends who resemble him superficially."

Williams glances in the backyard. Kalika was no longer there. "Would you mind if we looked around?" he asks.

"Do you have a search warrant?"

Williams is cagey. "We just stopped by to ask a few questions."

"Then I certainly do mind. Look, I live here with my boyfriend and a girlfriend. We're not kidnappers, and I resent your implying that we are."

Kent speaks for the first time. "Then why won't you let us look around?"

"That's my choice."

"What happened to your hand?" Kent asks, pointing to the bandage that covers Billy's second good swing at me.

"I cut it on a broken glass," I say.

"Hello?" Kalika says softly as she enters the living room from the direction of the hall, a towel tied around her waist over her bathing suit. "Is there a problem?"

"No," I say quickly. "These men were just leaving."

Williams stands and holds out the picture of Eric for Kalika to see. "Have you ever seen this young man?"

Kalika studies the photograph. Then looks my way with a cool smile. "Yes."

That's my daughter. She would talk about Billy next.

"Where did you see him?" Williams demands, casting me a hard look.

Kalika is thoughtful. "I can show you the place. It's not far from here. Would you like to take me there?"

I clear my throat. "That's not necessary."

"I don't mind," Kalika says. "It's not a problem."

I lower my head. Arguing with her in front of these men will not help.

"Don't be gone long," I say.

Kalika leaves with the officers. She doesn't even bother to change out of her suit. The men don't seem to mind. Kalika is more stunning than her mother, and they can't take their eyes off her. I pray they don't take their eyes off her, and that they don't have families. It is them I am worried about now.

Paula calls ten minutes after Kalika leaves.

She's in labor. I'll be there in two minutes, I promise.

Running out the door, Ray stops me. "Call us when the baby's been born."

I step past him. I haven't told him who was on the phone but I suppose it shows on my face. "I'll think about it."

He speaks to my back as I go down the steps. "Remember, you promised Kalika you would let her see the baby. Don't forget."

I ignore him, or wish I could.

15

Paula is having contractions in my car when I decide we are not going to the local hospital where her doctor is waiting. I turn left and head for the freeway. Paula is in pain, and in shock when I floor it.

"What are you doing?" she cries.

"I don't like your hospital," I say. "It's ill equipped. I'm taking you to a much nicer one. Don't worry, I have money, I'll pay."

"But they're expecting me! I called before I left!"

"It doesn't matter. This hospital is only thirty minutes away." It is actually over forty minutes away. "You'll like it, we can get you a room with a view of the mountains."

"But I'm not going on vacation! I'm going to have a baby! I don't need a room with a view!"

"It's always nice to have a view," I reply, patting her leg. "Don't worry, Paula, I know what I'm doing."

This baby—I don't know what's special about it. I don't know why Ray and Kalika are obsessed with it. But I do know they are the last people on earth who are going to see it.

The hospital I take her to, the famous Cedar Sinai, is surprised to see us. But the staff jumps to attention when I wave cash and gold credit cards in their faces. What a terrible thing it is that the quality of emergency care is often determined by money. Holding Paula's hand, I help her fill out the paperwork and then we are both ushered into a delivery room. The baby appears to be coming fast. A nurse asks me to put on a gown and a mask. She is nice, and lets me stay with Paula without asking questions.

Paula is now drenched in sweat and in the throes of *real* pain, which I have often been intimate with. An anesthesiologist appears and wants to give her Demerol to take the edge off the contractions, maybe an epidermal to partially numb her lower body. But Paula shakes her head.

"I don't need anything," she says. "I have my friend with me."

The anesthesiologist doesn't approve, but I am touched by the remark. I have become so human. Even sentimental nonsense has meaning to me. Paula's hand is sweaty in mine but I have seldom felt a softer touch.

"I am with you," I say. "I will stay with you."

The baby fakes us all out. It is eight hours later, at night, when the child finally makes an appearance—a handsome male of seven pounds five ounces, with more hair than most babies, and large blue eyes that I assume will fade to brown over the next few months. I am the first to hold the baby—other than the delivering physician—and I whisper in his ear the ancient mystical symbol that is supposed to remind the child of its true essence or soul.

"Vak," I say over and over again. It is practically the first sound the infant hears because he did not come out screaming, and the doctor and the others fell strangely silent at the moment of his birth. Indeed, it was almost as if time stood still for a moment.

Vak is a name for Saraswati, the Goddess of speech, the Mother above the head who brings the white light to saints and prophets. The baby smiles at me as I say Vak. Already, I think, I am in love with him. Wiping him gently off and handing him to Paula, I wonder who his father is.

"Is he all right?" she asks, exhausted from the effort but nevertheless blissful.

"Yes, he's perfect," I say, and laugh softly, feeling something peculiar in my words, an intuition, perhaps, of things to come and a life to be lived. "What are you going to call him?" I ask.

Paula cuddles her child near her face and the baby reaches out and touches her eyes. "I don't know," she says. "I have to think about it."

"Didn't you think about a name before?" a nurse asks.

Paula appears puzzled. "No. Never."

* * *

Death is a part of life. Calling home to see how Kalika has faired with the two police, I know the grave and the nursery sit on opposite sides of the same wall. That they are connected by a dark closet, where skeletons are hidden, and where the past is sometimes able to haunt the present. All who are born die, Krishna said. All who die will be reborn. Neither is supposed to be a cause for grief. Yet even I, with all my vast experience extending over fifty centuries, am not prepared for what is to happen next.

Kalika answers the phone. It is ten at night.

"Hello, Mother," she says.

"You knew it was me?"

"Yes."

"How are you? Did you just get home?"

"No. I have been home awhile. Where are you?"

I hesitate. "Ray must have told you."

"Yes. You're at the hospital?"

"Yes. How did you get on with the police?"

"Fine."

I have trouble asking the next question. "Are they all right?"

"You don't have to worry about them, Mother."

I momentarily close my eyes. "Did you kill them?"

Kalika is cool. "It is not your concern. The baby has been born. I want to see it."

How does she know the baby has been born? "No," I say. "Paula's still in labor. You can't see the baby now."

Kalika is a long time in responding. "What hospital are you at?"

"The local one. Let me speak to Ray a moment."

"Ray is not here. What is the name of this hospital?"

"But he seldom goes out. Are you sure he's not there?"

"He's not here. I'm telling you the truth, Mother. You will tell me the truth. What is the name of the hospital where you're at?"

Even as a human, I do not like to be pushed around. "All right, I will tell you. If you tell me why it is so important to you to see this baby?"

"You wouldn't understand."

"I gave birth to you. I am older than you know. I understand more than you think. Try me."

"It is not your concern."

"Fine. Then it is also not my concern to tell you where the child is. Let me speak to Ray."

Kalika speaks softly but there is tension in her words. "He's not here, I told you. I don't lie, Mother." She pauses. "But Eric is here."

I hear my heart pound. "What do you mean?"

"He's sitting on the couch beside me. He's still tied up but he's not gagged. Would you like to speak to him?"

I feel as if I stand on melting ice in a freezing river that flows into a black sea. A mist rises before me and the next moments are played out in shadow. There is no way I can second-guess Kalika because all of her actions—when judged by humans or vampires alike—are inexplicable. Perhaps it was a mistake to snap at her.

"Put him on," I say.

There is a moment of fumbling. It sounds as if my

daughter has momentarily covered the phone with her hand. Then the line is clear. Eric does not sound well.

"Hello?"

"Eric, it's me. Are you all right?"

He is breathing heavily, scared. "I don't know. She . . . This person says you have to tell her something or something bad will happen to me."

"Put her back on the line. Do it now!"

Another confused moment passes. But Eric remains on the line. "She doesn't want to talk to you. She says you have to tell me which hospital you're in. She says if you lie she will know it, and then something *really* bad will happen to me." Eric chokes with fear. "Could you tell her the name of the hospital? Please? This girl— She's so strong. She picked me up with one hand and carried me out here."

"Eric," I say, "try to convince her that I need to talk to her directly."

I hear Eric speaking to Kalika. But Eric is forced to stay on the line. I imagine his arms and legs still bound, Kalika holding the phone up to his ear. The tears in his eyes—I can see them in my mind, and I hear the many vows I swore to him.

"But I can promise you you're not going to die. I swear this to you, Eric, and I keep my word."

"You have to help me!" he cries. "She has long nails, and she says she's going to open the veins in my neck unless you tell her what hospital it is. Ouch! She's touching me!"

"Tell her the hospital is called St. Judes!"

"It's St. Judes!" he screams. Another soul-shattering pause. "She says you're lying! Oh God! Her nails!"

Sweat pours off my head. My heart is a jackhammer vibrating.

"Kalika!" I yell into the phone. "Talk to me!"

"She keeps shaking her head!" Eric weeps. "She's scratching my neck! Jesus help me!"

I fight to stay calm, and lose the fight. "Eric, shove the phone in her face!"

"Oh God, I'm bleeding! She's cut my neck! The blood is gushing out! Help me!"

"Eric, tell her I'll tell her the name of the hospital! Tell her!"

He begins to choke. "This can't be happening to me! I can't die! I don't want to die!"

Those are the last intelligible words he speaks. The rest—it goes on another two minutes—is slobbering sounds and pitiful weeping. It trails off into strangled gasps, then I must assume his heart has stopped beating. I sag against the wall of the hospital next to the place where the phone is attached. People stare at me from down the hall but I ignore them. Kalika lets me enjoy the silence. Another minute goes by before she returns to the phone.

"Then he should never have been born," she says calmly. "Is that what you wanted to tell him, Mother? Your famous quote."

I am in shock. "You," I whisper.

"I want to see the baby, Mother," she repeats.

"No."

"What is the name of the hospital? Where is it located?"

"I would never tell you!" I cry. "You're a monster!"

It is as if she smiles. I hear her unspoken mirth, somehow. Yet her voice remains flat. "And what are you? What did Krishna say to you about vampires in Kali Yuga?"

I can only assume Ray explained my dialogue with Krishna to Kalika. It doesn't matter—I am not in the mood for philosophical discussions. There is an aching void inside me that I had always believed a daughter would fill. Well, the irony is bitter, for the real Kali has always been described as the abyss, and now the void inside me feels as if it stretches forever. Eric's death screams continue to reverberate inside my skull.

"I am human now," I whisper. "I don't kill unless I have to."

"The same with me. This baby—you don't understand how I feel about it."

"How *you* feel about it? You have no feelings, Daughter."

"I will not argue. I will not repeat my questions. Answer now or you will regret it."

"I will never answer to you again."

Kalika doesn't hesitate. "There is someone else here I want you to speak with. He also sits on the couch beside me. But I have gagged him. Just a moment and I will remove his gag."

Oh no, I cringe. My demon child.

Seymour comes on the line. He strains to sound upbeat.

"Sita. What's happening?"

My voice is filled with agony. "What are you doing there?"

"Your daughter called me six hours ago. She said she needed to speak to me. I think Ray gave her my number. You remember Ray and I used to be friends when we were both normal high school kids? I caught the first plane down. Your daughter met me at the airport." He hesitates and probably glances at Eric's body. "She seemed really friendly at first."

"I told you not to come. I told you it was dangerous."

"Yeah, but I was worried about you."

"I understand. Is Ray there?"

"I haven't seen him." Seymour coughs and I hear his fear. There is talking in the background. "Your daughter says you're to tell me the name of the hospital where you are."

"Or something bad will happen to you?"

"She didn't say that exactly, but I think it would be safe to bet that will be the case." He pauses. "She seems to know when you're lying."

"She knows an awful lot." Yet Kalika is unable to "tune into" where I am. I find that curious, what with her incredible psychic abilities. "Tell her I want to talk to her."

I catch snatches of more mumbled conversation. Seymour remains on the line. "She says you are to tell me the name and location of the hospital." Seymour stops, and a note of desperation enters his voice. "What she did to Eric—you'd have to have been here. She made the old you look like a Girl Scout."

"I can imagine." I think frantically. "Tell her I'll make her a counter proposal. I'll bring the child to her in exactly twenty-four hours. At the end of the Santa Monica Pier at ten tomorrow night. Tell her if she so much as scratches you, she'll never see this baby, if she searches the entire globe."

Seymour relays my offer. Kalika appears to listen patiently. Then the phone is covered and I imagine my daughter is talking to Seymour. A minute goes by. Finally Seymour returns.

"She wants to know why you need twenty-four hours?"

"Because the baby has to remain in an incubator for a day. Tell her that's normal hospital procedure."

Seymour repeats what I say. He doesn't cover the phone this time but I still can't hear Kalika speak— her voice is too soft. I tire of this game. But there is a reason why my daughter doesn't let me talk to her directly at critical times. It heightens my helplessness, and her strategy says a lot about how her mind works. She is a master manipulator. I have as much hope for the two missing police officers as I do for Eric. Seymour finally relays her latest message.

"She says you are lying about the incubator but she doesn't care," he says. "As long as you bring the baby, she will wait to meet you."

"She has to bring you as well," I say. "Alive."

Seymour acts cheerful. "I made that a condition of the bargain."

"Does she know where the Santa Monica Pier is?"

"We both know where it is, in Santa Monica."

I try to sound optimistic. "Hang lose, Seymour. I'll get you out of this mess somehow."

He pauses. "Do what you have to, Sita."

Kalika must have taken the phone from him. It goes dead.

16 ~~~

Midnight has arrived, the witching hour. I stand in a clean hallway and stare through the glass at the newborn babies in their incubators. There are six— they all look so innocent, especially Paula's. A pediatric nurse busies herself with the infants, checking their temperatures and heartbeats, drawing blood. She sees me peering through the glass, and I must look like a sight because she comes to the door and asks if I'm all right. I shuffle over to her.

"Yeah, I was just wanting to hold my friend's baby again. Before I leave the hospital." I add, "I'm not sure when I'll be able to come back."

The nurse is sweet. "I saw you earlier with the mother. Put on a gown and mask and you can hold him. I'll get you the stuff. Which one is he?"

"Number seven."

"He doesn't have a name?"

"Not yet."

Soon I am dressed appropriately and I am led into the newborns. I watch as the nurse draws blood from Paula's baby and places the vial in a plastic rack, with the other vials. *Ramirez* is all she writes on the white label. The nurse hands me number seven to hold.

"He's so beautiful," she says.

"Yeah. He takes after his mother."

It is good to hold the baby after the shock I have been through. Somehow the nearness of the child soothes me. I stare into his lovely blue eyes and laugh when he seems to smile at me. He is full of life; he kicks the whole time, tries to reach up and touch me with his tiny hands. It is almost as if I am his mother, I treasure him so.

"Why couldn't this have been my child?" I whisper.

Of course I had prayed for a daughter.

Ten minutes later, when the nurse is prepared to leave, she says I can take the baby to Paula's room if I want. The nurse has her back to me as she speaks.

"I'll do that," I say.

"I'll come check the child again in an hour," she says, working with the last baby on her rotation. I turn toward the door.

"I'll tell Paula," I say.

Then I stop and stare at the vials of blood. Warm red blood—it has been the center of my life for five thousand years. Perhaps that is why I halt. I want to be near it, to smell it, to enjoy its dark color. Yet a part of me has doubts. There is *something* about this blood in particular—number seven's—that draws me. It is almost as if the red liquid hypnotizes me. Hardly thinking, I remove the vial from its plastic rack and slip it into my pocket. The nurse doesn't look over.

I take the baby to Paula.

She is sitting up and praying when I enter, a rosary in her hands. Standing silently at the door, I watch her for a full minute. There is something about how she focuses as she prays. She projects an intensity and at the same time an ease that baffles me. She hardly speaks above a whisper but it is as if her words fill the room. "Our Father, who art in heaven . . ."

"Hello," I say finally. "I brought you a present."

Paula is pleased. But she only smiles as I hand her the child. The boy is wise—he immediately searches for and finds her right nipple. I sit by Paula's bed in the dim room. The window is open, we are high up. The city lights spread out beneath us like a haze of jewels and dust. Seymour never leaves my thoughts, nor does Eric. I have twenty-two hours left to do the impossible.

"How do you feel?" I ask.

"Wonderful. I'm hardly sore at all. Isn't he adorable?"

"If he was any more adorable we would do nothing else but stand around and admire him."

"Thank you for staying with me."

"Are you still mad that I brought you here?"

Paula is puzzled. "I like this hospital, but why did you bring me here?"

I lean forward. "I'd like to answer that question honestly because I lied to you before, and I think you know it. I'll tell you in a few minutes. But before I do, may I ask about this child's father?"

Paula appears troubled. "Why do you ask?"

"Because of your precise reaction right now. The day I met you, you reacted in the same way when I asked about the father." I pause. "I really would like to hear how you got pregnant."

Paula tries to brush me off. "Oh, I think it was in the usual way."

"Was it?"

Paula studies me. Even though she is feeding her baby, her gaze is shrewd. It is ironic that she pays me precisely the same compliment.

"You're perceptive, Alisa," she says. "I noticed that the day we met. You miss nothing. Have you always been this way?"

"For a long time."

Paula sighs and looks out the window at the city lights. "This is called the City of Angels. It would take an angel to believe what I have to say next. The priest at St. Andrews didn't believe me. I told him my whole story one day, in confession. He ordered me to do ten Hail Marys." She adds, "That's a huge penance."

"It must be a great story."

Paula shakes her head. "It's a confusing story. I hardly know where to begin."

"At the beginning. That's always easiest."

Paula continues to stare out the window, while her

child suckles her breast. "I grew up in an orphanage—I told you that—and was alone most of my life, even when I was surrounded by people. I purposely lived in my own world because my whole environment seemed harsh to me. But I wasn't what you would call unhappy. I often experienced moments of unusual joy and happiness. I could see a flower or a butterfly, or even just a tree, and become joyful. Sometimes the joy would become so strong I would swoon. A few times I lost track of where I was, what I was doing. When that happened I was taken to the doctor by the woman who ran my orphanage. They did all kinds of tests and I was given a grim diagnosis."

"Epilepsy," I say.

Paula is surprised. "How did you know?"

I shrug. "Saint Paul and Joan of Arc have since been diagnosed as epileptic because they had visions and heard voices. It's the current fad diagnosis for mystics—past and present. I'm sorry, please continue."

"I didn't know that. I just knew that at the moments I was most alive, I had trouble maintaining normal consciousness. But when I swooned it wasn't like I passed out. The opposite—I felt as if I was transported to a vast realm of beauty and light. Only it was all inside me. I couldn't share it with anyone. These experiences went on throughout my childhood and teens. They invoked in me a sense of . . . This is hard to explain."

"When you swooned you felt close to God," I say.

"Yes, exactly. I felt a sacred presence. And I found,

as I got older, that if I prayed for long periods the trances would come over me. But I didn't pray for them to happen. I prayed because I wanted to pray. I wanted to think of God, nothing else. It was the only thing that completely satisfied me." She paused. "Does that sound silly?"

"No. I often think of God. Go on."

"It gets bizarre now. You have to forgive me ahead of time." She pauses. "I love the desert. I love to drive deep into it all by myself. Especially Joshua National Park—I love those tall trees. They stand out there in the middle of nowhere like guards, their arms up, so patient. I feel like they're protecting the rest of us somehow. Anyway I was out there nine months ago, by myself, near sunset. I was sitting on a bluff watching the sun go down and it was incredibly beautiful—the colors, the clouds shot through with red and orange and purple. It looked like a rainbow made out of sand and sun. The air was so silent I thought I could hear an ant walking. I had been there all day and as soon as it was dark I was going to head back to town. But as the sun vanished beneath the horizon I lost track of time, as I had done often before."

"But this time was different?" I ask.

"Yes. It was as if I just blinked and then it became pitch-black. The sky was filled with a million stars. They were so bright! I could have been in outer space. I can't exaggerate this—they were so bright they weren't normal. It was almost as if I had been transported to another world, inside a huge star cluster, and was looking up at its nighttime sky."

"You were completely awake all this time?"

"Yes. I was happy but I hadn't lost awareness of my surroundings. I could still see the Joshua trees."

"But you had lost awareness of a big chunk of time?"

"It was more like the time lost me. Anyway, something else started to happen. While I marveled over the stars, the blue one directly above me began to glow extremely bright. It was as if it were moving closer to the earth, toward me, and I felt afraid. It got so bright I was blinded. I had to close my eyes. But I could still feel it coming. I could feel its heat. It was roasting me alive!"

"Were you in pain?"

Paula struggled for words. "I was overwhelmed is a better way to put it. A high-pitched sound started to vibrate the area. Remember, I had my eyes closed but I could still see the light and knew that it was growing more intense. The rays of the star pierced my eyelids. The sound pierced my ears. I wanted to scream—maybe I was screaming. But I don't think I was in actual physical pain. It was more as if I were being transformed."

"Transformed? Into what?"

"I don't know. That's just the impression I had at the time. That somehow this light and heat and sound were changing me."

"What happened next?"

"I blacked out."

"That's it?"

"There's more. The next thing I knew it was morning and I was lying on the bluff with the sun shining in my eyes. My whole body ached and I was incredibly thirsty. Also, my exposed skin was slightly red, as if I had been burned." She stopped.

"What is it?"

"You won't believe this."

"I'll believe anything if I believe what you just told me. Tell me"

Paula glanced at me. "Do you believe me?"

"Yes. But tell me what you wanted to say."

"The Joshua trees around me—they were all taller."

"Are you sure?"

"Quite sure. Some were twice the size they had been the evening before."

"Interesting. Could you take me to this spot someday?"

"Sure. But I haven't been back to it since."

"Why not?" I ask, although I know why.

Paula takes a deep breath and looks down at her son. "Because six weeks after this happened I learned I was pregnant." She chuckled to herself. "Pretty weird, huh?"

"Only if you weren't having sex with someone at the time."

"I wasn't."

"Are you a virgin?" I ask.

"No. But I didn't have a boyfriend at that time. Not even around that time. You must think I'm mad."

"I don't know," I say. "A few times in my life aliens have swooped down and tried to get me to go to bed with them."

"I didn't see a flying saucer," Paula says quickly.

"I was joking. I know you didn't." I am thoughtful.

"Did you have any other unusual symptoms after this incident? Besides being pregnant?"

Paula considers. "I've had colorful dreams for the past few months. They're strong—they wake me up."

"What are they about?"

"I can never remember them clearly. But there are always stars in them. Beautiful blue stars, like the ones I saw out in the desert."

I think of the dreams I've had of Krishna.

"What do you think this all means?" I ask.

She is shy. "I haven't the faintest idea."

"You must have a theory?" I ask.

"No. None."

"Do you think you were raped while you lay unconscious in the desert?"

Paula considers. "That would be the logical explanation. But even though I was sore when I woke up, I wasn't sore down there."

"But is it possible you were raped?"

"Yes. I was out cold. Anything could have happened to me during that time."

"Were your clothes disturbed in any way?"

"They were— They felt different on me."

"What do you mean?"

Paula hesitates. "My belt felt tighter."

"Like it had been removed, and then put back on, only a notch tighter?"

Paula lowers her head. "Yes. But I honestly don't think I was raped."

"Do you think you had an epileptic attack?"

"No. I don't think I have epilepsy. I don't believe that diagnosis anymore."

"But you believe Joshua trees stand guard over us? Like angels?"

She smiles. "Yeah. I am a born believer."

Her smile is so kind, so gentle. It reminds me of Radha's, Krishna's friend. I make my decision right then. Leaning forward and speaking seriously, I make Paula jump by the change in my tone.

"I have some bad news for you, Paula. I want you to brace yourself and I want you to listen to me with as open a mind as I have listened to you. Can you do this?"

"Sure. What's wrong?"

"There are two people I know who—for reasons I do not fully understand yet—want your baby."

Paula is stunned. "What do they want it for?"

"I don't know. But I do know that one of these people—the young woman—is a killer." My eyes burn and I have trouble keeping my voice steady. "She killed a friend of mine two hours ago."

"Alisa! This can't be true. Who is this woman?"

I shake my head. "She is someone so powerful, so brilliant, so cruel—that there is no point in going to the police and explaining what happened."

"But you have to go to the police. If a murder has been committed, they must be told."

"The police cannot stop her. I cannot stop her. She wants your baby. She is looking for him now and when she comes here for him you won't be able to stop her." I pause. "You are my friend, Paula. We haven't known each other long but I believe friendship is not based on time. I think you know I'm your friend and that I would do anything for you."

Paula nods. "I know that."

"Then you must do something for me now. You must leave this hospital tonight, with your son. I have money, lots of money I can give you. You must go to a place far from here, and not even tell *me* where it is."

I am talking too fast for Paula. "Is this the reason you took me to this hospital?"

"Yes. They thought you were going to the local one. But they know you've given birth to a baby somewhere in this city. They're clever—they'll check all the hospitals in the city to see where you're registered. Eventually they'll locate you."

"You spoke of a young woman. Who is the other person?"

I am stricken with grief. "My boyfriend."

"Ray?"

"Yes. But he's not the Ray I once knew." I lower my head. "I can't talk about him now. It is the girl who's the danger—she's only twenty. Her name is Kalika. Please believe me when I tell you there is literally no one who can stop her when she sets her mind on something."

"But how can she be so powerful?" Paula protests.

I stare at her. "She was just born that way. You see, she wasn't born under normal circumstances. Like your son, there's a mystery surrounding her birth, her conception even."

"Tell me about it."

"I can't. You wouldn't believe me if I did."

"But I would. You believed me."

"Only because I have gone through strange times in

my life. But Kalika transcends anything I've ever encountered. Her psyche *burns* through all obstacles. She could be on her way here now. I swear to you, if she gets here before you get away, your child will die."

Paula doesn't protest. She is strangely silent. "I was warned," she says.

It is my turn to be stunned. "Who warned you?"

"It came in a dream."

"But you said you didn't remember any of your dreams."

"I remember this one. I was standing on a wide field and this old man with white hair and a crooked grin walked up to me and said something that didn't make sense. Until right now."

"What was it?" I ask.

"He said, 'Herod was an evil king who didn't get what he wanted. But he knew where the danger lay.' Then the old man paused and asked me, 'Do you know where the danger lies, Paula?'" She stops and looks once more at her child, we both look at him. "It was an odd dream."

"Yes." My heart is heavy with anxiety. "Will you leave?"

Paula nods. "Yes. I trust you. But why can't I tell you where I'm going?"

"This girl, this Kalika—I fear she could rip the information from my mind."

Paula cringes. "But I must have a way to get hold of you."

"I will give you a special number. You call it a month from now and leave your name and number.

But don't tell me where you are. Wait until you talk to me—until you are certain it is me—to tell me that. That is very important."

Paula is worried for me. "Are you in danger?"

I lean back and momentarily close my eyes. My greatest task is still before me and I am exhausted. If only I had my old powers. *If*—the most annoying word in the English language.

But what if I was powerful again?

Powerful as a vampire?

Seymour would not have to die, nor would I.

But my daughter would die. Perhaps.

"Don't worry, I have a protector," I tell Paula. "This wonderful man I once met—he promised to protect me if I did what he said. And he was someone capable of keeping his promises."

Of course I don't tell her that I have disobeyed Krishna many times.

17

Arturo's alchemy of transformation works by having the substance of what one wishes to become vibrate at a high level in one's aura. To become human, I took Seymour's blood and placed it—above my head—in a clear vial the sun shone through while I lay on a copper plate surrounded by specially arranged magnets and crystals. Only Arturo knew how to use these tools fully. The New Age is still centuries behind his knowledge. The proponents of New Age mysticism hold quartz crystals or amethysts and relax some, but Arturo could use these minerals to attain enlightenment, or even immortality. His only weakness was that he strove for immortality with a vampire for a girlfriend. He was a priest and erroneously thought I could give him the equivalent of the blood of Jesus.

His blasphemy was his sin, and his eventual ruin. He tried to use me, betrayed me. But he is dead now and I mourn him.

To become a vampire again, I need a source of vampire blood.

I lied to Seymour, naturally. There is one possible source—Yaksha. Yet I have sunk Yaksha's body in the sea and will never be able to locate it, not without the powers of a vampire. Still, there is one other possible source of his blood, besides that in his body. Eddie Fender kept Yaksha captive in an ice-cream truck for several weeks, kept him cold and weak. It was from this very ice-cream truck that I eventually rescued Yaksha, who had no legs and hardly any lower torso. He bled in that truck and his blood must still be there, frozen and preserved.

But that truck was parked on the street in the vicinity of a warehouse I burned down to kill Eddie and his crew of vampires. That was approximately two months ago. The chances that the truck will still be there are slim. The police will almost certainly have confiscated it, towed it off to some forsaken lot. Yet I hurry to the dirty street in the poor part of town on the off chance that I can uncover a bloody Popsicle. Desperate people do desperate things.

And the ice truck is still there. Wow.

A homeless man with white hair and a grimy face sits in his rags near the driver's door. He has a shopping cart loaded with aluminum cans and blankets that look as if they were woven during the Depression. He is thin and bent but he looks up at me with bright eyes as I approach. He sits on the curb, nursing a small carton of milk. I immediately reach for my money. It is his lucky night. I will give him a hundred and tell him to hit the road. But something in his voice gives me reason to pause. His greeting is peculiar.

"You look very nice tonight," he says. "But I know you're in a hurry."

I stand above him and glance around. There is no one visible, but it is the middle of the night and this ghetto is a wonderful place to get raped or killed. Last time I was here I had to rough up a couple of cops. They thought I was a hooker, and one of them wanted to arrest me. I study the homeless man.

"How do you know I'm in a hurry?" I ask.

He grins and his smile is much brighter than I would have anticipated. Bright like his eyes even though he is covered in dirt.

"I know a few things," he says. "You want this truck I suppose. I've been guarding it for you."

I laugh softly. "I appreciate that. I have a horrible craving for an ice-cream bar right now."

He nods. "The refrigerator unit still works. I've kept it serviced."

I'm impressed. "You're handy with tools?"

"I have fixed a thing or two in my day." He offers me his hand. "Please help me up. My bones are old and sore, and I have been waiting here for you for such a long time."

I help him—I don't mind a little dirt. "How long have you been here?"

He brushes himself off, but ends up making a worse mess of his torn clothes. He blinks at my question as if

I have confused him, although he does not smell of alcohol. He finishes his carton of milk and sets the empty container in his shopping cart.

"I don't rightly know," he says finally. "I think I've been here since you were last here."

I pause, feeling an odd sensation coursing through my body. But I dismiss it. I have too much on my mind to waste precious minutes with an old man in the middle of the night.

"I haven't been here in a couple of months," I say, reaching in my pocket. "Look, can I give you . . ."

"Then I must have been here that long," he interrupts. "I knew you'd come back."

I stop with my hand wrapped around a few twenties. "I don't know what you're talking about," I say quietly.

He grins a crooked grin. "I don't need your money." He turns and shuffles up the street. "You do what you have to do. No one can blame you for not trying hard."

I stare at him as he fades into the night.

Such a strange old guy. He left his shopping cart behind.

I wonder what his name was.

The rear compartment of the truck is locked, but I break it with a loose brick. Actually, I could have sworn that I broke the lock the last time I entered it. The interior is ice cold as I squeeze inside, a flashlight in my hand.

Just inside the door is a puddle of frozen blood.

I slip a nail under it and pull up the whole red wafer at once. Shining my flashlight through the frosted glass, I feel a surge of tremendous power. I hold in my hands immortality, and I feel as if Krishna saved this blood just so I'd find it. Back in my own car, I break the ice into small pieces and let them melt in a stainless-steel thermos.

Now I must return to Las Vegas. If it were not the middle of the night, I would fly, but driving it will have to be—at least four hours of pushing the speed limit. Also, I have to worry that Arturo's house is being watched by government agents. From reading the papers, I know the dust has not settled from the nuclear explosion in the desert. They must think I am dead, but will not assume that I am. There is an important difference.

The rays of the sun will power my transformation. What is crucial is that I have most of the day to complete the transformation back to becoming a vampire, if it is possible. There is a chance I will end up like Ralphe, a bloodthirsty ghoul. But I have no choice except to risk the alchemist's ancient experiment. To give up my hard-sought humanity will be bitter, yet I have to admit a part of me craves my old power. It will be nice to confront my daughter one on one and not tremble in my shoes.

Yet I intend to tremble, especially if I am a vampire.

She will not know until too late who it is she faces.

18

The drive to Las Vegas is more pleasant than I anticipated. There is something about roaring along a dark empty road that relaxes me. Keeping an eye out for police, I set the cruise control at an even eighty. It seems only a short while before the horizon begins to glow with the polluted lake of colored neon that is the gambling capital of the world. I will roll the red dice today, I think, and pray for a successful combination of DNA. The eastern sky is already warm with light. The sun will rise soon.

I park a block down the street from Arturo's house and scan the area for FBI agents, cops, or army personnel. But the place appears quiet, forgotten in the fallout of the incinerated army base. Slipping over Arturo's back fence, I am through an open window and into the house in less than a minute. An eight-and-a-half-by-eleven photograph stands in a cheap frame on the kitchen table—Arturo and me, taken one night while we were out on the Strip together. When I believed he was a down-on-his-luck government employee and he thought I was a sucker. The picture gives me reason to pause. I pick it up and study Arturo's features. They remind me so much of someone I know.

"You are Kalika's father," I whisper, stunned.

Everything makes sense in an instant. Vampires are sterile, with one another, with human partners. But Arturo was neither a vampire nor a human. He was a hybrid, forged in the Middle Ages, a combination of the two, and I slept with him in a Las Vegas hotel room just before he betrayed me to the government. I was pregnant from before the transformation. In other words, I was still a vampire when Kalika was conceived. Yet she is partially human, and that no doubt explains her lack of sensitivity to the sun. She is the result of a queer toss of the genetic dice, and perhaps that's what it took for a soul of her dark origin to incarnate on earth.

And I assumed Ray was her father.

I'm aware of him at my back even before he speaks.

"I'm surprised you didn't guess earlier," he says.

I turn, still holding the photograph. Ray remains hidden in the shadows, appropriately enough. It is not just Kalika's birth that I suddenly understand. But my new insights, which are not entirely clear to me yet, are ill-defined ghosts that refuse to enter the living body of logical reason. Despair and denial engulf me.

I feel as if I stand in a steaming graveyard with a tombstone at my back. The death date of the corpse is carved in the future, the name scribbled in blood that will never dry. I know the truth but refuse to look at it.

And there is a mirror on this tombstone.

Covered with a faint film of black dust.

"You could have told me," I say.

"I could only tell you what you wanted to hear."

The weakness of grief spreads through my limbs. Ray has become a travesty to me, someone I cannot bear to look at, yet I don't want him to go away. He is all I have left. The graveyard in my mind is littered with hidden mines. I fear that if I move or speak to him, one might explode and toss a skeleton in my lap.

"How did you get here?" I ask.

"You brought me here."

"Does Kalika know I'm here?"

"I don't think so. But she might."

"You didn't tell her?"

"No."

Putting down the photograph, I take a moment to collect myself. My imagined graveyard falls away beneath me as the tombstone collapses. Yet I am forced to remain standing in this house where Arturo once lived.

"Can I ask you a question?" I say finally.

He remains in the shadows. "Don't ask anything you don't want answered."

"But I do want answers."

He shakes his head. "Few really want the complete truth. It doesn't matter if you're a vampire or a human. The truth is overrated, and too often painful." He adds, "Let it be, Sita."

There is emotion in my voice. "I need to know just one thing."

"No," he warns me. "Don't do this to yourself."

"Just one little thing. I understand how you found me in Las Vegas. You explained that and it made sense to me, but you never explained how you picked up my trail again in Los Angeles. While I was driving here, you should have been in the basement in this house, changing back into a human."

"It was dark that night," he says.

His answer confuses me. "It's dark every night."

"It would have been dark in the basement."

The confusion passes. "You need the sun to power the alchemy."

"Yes."

"You must still be a vampire?"

"No."

"You must have followed us to L.A.?"

"No."

"Who are you? What did Eddie's blood do to you?"

"Nothing. Eddie's blood never touched me."

"But you said—"

"I lied," he interrupts. "You asked me to lie to you. You do not want the truth. You swear to yourself that you do but you swear at the altar of false gods. Let it be, Sita. We can leave this place together. It can be as it once was between us, if you will just let it. It is all up to you."

"You are not ready to hear."

"When will I be ready to hear?"

"Soon."

"You know this?"

"I know many things, Mother."

"Why is it all up to me?" I ask. "You're as responsible for what happened to us as I am."

"No."

"Stop saying no! Stop saying yes! Explain yourself!"

He is a long time answering. "What do you want me to say?"

I place my hands on the sides of my head. "Just tell me who you are. Why you are not like the old Ray. How you found me in the coffee shop." I feel so weak. "Why you knocked at my door."

"When did I knock at your door?"

"Here." I point. "You knocked at that door right there. You said it was you."

"When did I knock at your door?" he repeats.

Of course I have not answered his question. He is asking about time, and I am talking about place. I have to force my next words into the air where they can be heard and understood.

"You appeared right after I changed into a human," I say.

"Yes."

"You're saying that's a remarkable coincidence."

"I am saying you should stop now."

I nod to myself, speak to myself. "You are saying the two events are related; the transformation and your reappearance. That you only reentered my life because I had become human."

"Close."

I pause. "What am I missing?"

"Everything."

"But you just said I was close!"

"When you roll the dice, close does not count. You either win or you lose."

"What did I lose when you returned?"

"*What* is not important. *Why* is all that matters."

"*Now listen to my song. It dispels all illusions . . . When you feel lost remember me, and you will see that the things you desire most are the very things that bring you the greatest sorrow.*"

"I have always desired two things," I say, remembering the Lord's words. "For five thousand years I have desired them. They were the two things that were taken from me the night Yaksha came for me and made me a vampire. The night he stole my daughter and husband. I never saw either of them again."

Ray is sympathetic. "I know."

I hang my head and it is now me who stands in shadows. "But when you came into my life I felt as if Rama had been returned to me. And when I became human and thought I was pregnant with your baby, I felt as if Krishna had returned Lalita to me." There is a tear on my face, maybe two, and I have to stop and take a deep breath. "But it didn't work that way. The things I craved so long were my greatest illusions. And they have brought me the greatest sorrow."

"Yes."

I lift my head and stare at him.

"They are not real," I say.

"Yes."

"As a vampire, I could see through my illusions, and that kept me going all these years, but as a human

I couldn't see what was real and what wasn't. I was too weak."

"You create what you want. You always have. If you don't like it, you can always leave."

He speaks with gentle passion. "Don't say it, Sita."

But I have to. I feel as if I can see through him. Now I understand why he never went out. Why he never met my friends or spoke to anyone besides Kalika and me. Why I had to do everything with my own hands. Between us, they were the only pair of hands we had.

"You're not real," I say.

He steps out of the shadows. His face is so beautiful.

"It doesn't matter, Sita. We can pretend it doesn't matter. I don't want to leave you."

My body is a chalice of misery. "But you're dead," I moan.

He comes close enough to touch me. "It doesn't matter."

No tears fall from my face. Dry sobs rack my body. They are worse than moist tears, worse because they are the evidence of evaporated grief, and I have only these to show to this silhouette of a boyfriend who stands before me now. This lover who can only love me as I deem myself worthy. No wonder he turned against me when I turned against him. He is a mirror on the tombstone. The film of black dust clears, and I see in the mirror that I have slowly been burying myself since I first came up the stairs of this house and heard the knock at the front door.

Who is it? Your darling. Open the door.

"I can't keep this door open," I whisper.

He touches my lower lip. "Sita."

I turn my head away from his hand. "No. You must go back."

"To where?"

"To where you came from."

"That is the abyss. There is nothing there. I am not there."

A note of quiet hysteria enters my voice. "You're not here. You're worse than a ghost. No one can see you! How can I possibly love you?"

He grabs my hand. "But you feel me. You know I'm here."

I fight to shake free of his hand but I just end up gripping it tighter. Yet I do not press it to my heart, as I used to. His hand is cold.

"No," I say. "I know you're not here."

He lightly kisses my finger. "Do you feel that?"

"No."

"You lie."

"You are the lie! You don't exist! How can I make you cease to exist!"

My words wound him, finally—they seem to tear the very fabric of his existence. For a moment his face shimmers, then goes out of focus. Yet he draws in a sudden breath and his warm brown eyes lock on to my eyes. He is not merely a mirror, but a hologram from a dimension where there are more choices than time and space. He is the ultimate *maya,* the complete illusion. The perfect love dressed in my own grief. No wonder when I met him in the coffee shop he was wearing the clothes he died in. He is nothing but a memory shouted back down the tunnel all mortals pass through when they leave this world. Yes, Ray is dead but I have let him become my own death as well.

He seems to read my thoughts.

His hope fades. He answers my last question.

"I died a vampire," he says. "You must kill me the way you would kill a vampire." He grabs a knife from the nearby table and presses it into my hand. "My heart beats only for you."

He wants me to cut his heart out. I try to push him away, but he holds me close. I can feel his breath on my face, like the brush of a winter wind. Yet now, here at the end, his eyes burn with a strange red light, the same light I have occasionally glimpsed in my daughter's eyes. He nods again as he reads my mind.

"If I return to the abyss," he says, "I'll see Kali there." He squeezes the handle of the knife into my palm. "Do it quick. You're right, the love is gone. I do want to die."

"I should never have been born," I whisper, addressing his last remark.

He manages a faint smile "Goodbye, Sita."

I stab him in the heart. I cut his flesh and his bones, and the blood gushes over my hands, onto my clothes, and over the floor. The black blood of the abyss, the empty space of Kali. But I scream as I kill him, scream to God for mercy, and the knife mysteriously falls from my hand and bounces on the dry floor. The blood evaporates.

His heart no longer beats and I'm no longer bloody.

He is gone, my ancient love is gone.

Out the window, the sun rises.

Taking Yaksha's blood, I pour it into the vial that

once held Seymour's blood, the clear vial that I place above the copper and the crystals, between the cross-shaped magnets and the shiny mirror that reflects the rays of the sun directly into Arturo's hidden basement. I recline on the copper and the alchemy begins to work its dark magic on my trembling body. I have to wonder exactly *what* I will be when the sun finally sets and the process is complete. On impulse I have added to the vial a few drops of blood from Paula's child. The blood of the infant that Kalika covets above all else.

I can only hope it does me good.

19 ━━━➤

Eight o'clock that evening I sit in the living room of Mr. and Mrs. Hawkins, in the very house Eric longed to return to until his throat was cut. Eric's parents are younger than I would have guessed. Mr. Hawkins can be no more than forty-two and I doubt his wife has reached forty. They must have married young and had Eric when they were barely out of their teens. He is stern faced, but it is a practiced expression, one he wears for his patients. But I see his intelligence and natural curiosity beneath it. She is plump and kindly, fussing with her hands as she constantly thinks of her son. She wears her heart on her face, her eyes are red from constant crying. Their address was in the phone book.

I just knocked at their door and told them I have information concerning their missing son. They invited me in because I am young and pretty and look as if I could harm no one. They sit across from me and wait for me to speak. There is no easy way to say it.

"Your son is dead," I say. "He was murdered last night. I thought you would want to know rather than to be left wondering. Before I leave here, I'll give you the address where his body can be found. He's in a house not far from here." I pause. "I'm truly sorry to have to bring you this information. It must be a great shock to both of you."

Mrs. Hawkins bursts into gasping sobs and buries her face in her hands. Mr. Hawkins's nostrils flare with anger. "How do you know this?" he demands.

"As you look at me you must see that I match the description of the young woman who picked up Eric in the park. I am, in fact, that person. But I am not the one who killed your son. On the contrary, I fought hard to save him. I'm very sorry I failed. Eric was a sweet boy. I liked him quite a lot."

They are in turmoil, which is inevitable. "This can't be true," Mr. Hawkins stammers.

"It is true. You will verify that for yourself when you go to the house. But I would rather you sent the police ahead of you. Eric died from a serious throat wound." I add reluctantly, "Just before I came here I tried to clean up, but there is still a lot of blood."

Mrs. Hawkins continues to sob. Mr. Hawkins leans forward in his chair, his skin flushed with blood, his face quivering with fury. "Who are you?" he asks.

"My name is not important. It's true I kidnapped your son but I meant him no harm. I do understand that you won't believe me. That you must hate me. If the situation were reversed I would probably hate you. But I can give you nothing to identify me with, and after I leave here, you will never see me again. The police will never find me."

Mr. Hawkins snorts. "You're not leaving this house, young lady. I'm calling the police as soon as I'm through with you."

"You should call the police. I've written down the address you need on a piece of paper." I take the scrap and hand it to him. He frowns as he glances at the slip. I continue, "I can give you directions to the house, but I must warn you two police officers who were there yesterday were also killed. Or rather, I must assume they were killed because they went off with the same person who killed your son and they didn't come back."

I add this last remark because I'm puzzled that no one has been to the house searching for them. When I stopped by half an hour earlier, looking for Kalika and Seymour, I could find no sign that the place had been examined by the authorities. Especially since Eric was still lying on the couch in all his gore. It was not pleasant trying to clean him up. He looked as if he had died in agony, which, of course, he had.

"You are talking a bunch of trash," Mr. Hawkins snaps.

"I am telling you the truth," I reply simply.

Mrs. Hawkins finally comes up for air. "Why did this person kill my boy?"

"To try to force me to reveal the whereabouts of a newborn baby. The person who murdered your son is obsessed with this child. She would do anything to get to him. But I refused to give her the information she needed, so Eric was killed." I pause. "None of these facts are important to you. None of them will make any sense to you. But I do want you to know that when I leave this house, I am going to meet with this young woman, and I am going to do everything in my power to stop her. I know you'll want revenge for what has happened to your son, or at the very least justice. I will try to give you both tonight, and keep this person from murdering again." I stand suddenly. "Now I have to go."

"You're not going anywhere!" Mr. Hawkins shouts as he tries to rise. But before his bottom can leave the chair, I effortlessly hold him down with one hand. My strength startles him.

"Please," I say gently. "You can't keep me here. It's not possible. And you won't be able to follow me. Just know that your son was brave and that forces beyond our control conspired to end his life before it should have ended. Try to understand his death as an act of God's will. I try to see it that way."

I leave them then quickly. They hardly have a chance to react, and later they will both wonder if my visit was a dream. But I know they will go straight to the house after they call the police. I know they will see their dead son before anyone else does. They loved him, and they should be the ones to close his eyes.

My car is around the block. Soon I am in it and driving for the ocean. There is an appointment I have with destiny and my daughter. I don't know which I trust less.

20

The transformation has worked and I am indeed a vampire again. Yet I am different, in a variety of ways, from what I was before. It was largely Yaksha's blood that filtered the sun's rays into my aura, and no doubt that is the main reason for the great increase in my strength. If I could jump fifty feet in the air before, I can leap a hundred now. If I could hear a leaf break and fall a mile away, now I can hear an ant crawl from its hole at twice that distance. My sense of smell is a wonder; the night air is an encyclopedia of fragrant information to me. And my eyes are like lasers. Not only can I see much farther than before, I feel the fire in my gaze, and I seriously doubt if even Kalika can withstand the power of it.

Yet these refinements are not confined to strength

and power. There is something else that has entered my life, something that I have never known before. I don't even have a word for it. I just feel—lucky, as if good fortune will smile on me. A white star seems to shine over my head, or maybe it is blue. I have to wonder if this is the effect of what I added to Yaksha's blood.

I am confident as I race toward the pier.

Santa Monica Beach, by the pier, is deserted as I drive up. I find that fact curious; it is, after all, only ten in the evening. The night is cold, true, but I have to wonder if there is another force at work. It is almost as if a psychic cloud hangs over the area, a fog of *maya* wrapped in astral matter. I clearly sense the force and my confidence wavers. For only my daughter could create it, and it is like nothing I have ever seen before. It seems to suck up life itself, which is why people have shunned the place. As I park my car down the block from the pier, I see not a soul. They may all be in their homes, trying to explain to their children that nightmares are not real. I myself feel as if I'm moving through a dream. My newly regained powers are physically exhilarating, but my dread of confronting Kalika is a heavy burden.

I see them, the two of them, at the end of the pier.

Seymour is looking out to sea. Kalika is nearby, in a long white dress, feeding the birds crumbs of bread. I am a half mile distant yet I see their every feature. Seymour pretends to be enjoying the view but he keeps glancing at Kalika. The muscles in his neck are tight; he is scared. Yet he appears unhurt and I am grateful for that.

Kalika is a mystery. There is an almost full moon, which shines through her long black hair like silver dust blowing on a black wind. As she feeds the birds, she is fully focused on them as if nothing else has greater meaning to her. This is a quality I have noticed in Kalika before. When she is doing something, nothing else occupies her mind. No doubt when she opened Eric's throat she was with him a hundred percent. It is a sobering thought given the fact that she has a hostage beside her. Kali and her string of skulls. Will my daughter have three fresh ones to add to her necklace before the night is over?

I think of Paula, who caught a cab from the hospital. Running out into the night with twenty thousand dollars in cash and a beautiful baby boy wrapped in a hospital receiving blanket. All because a new friend told her she was in danger. Then again, she had her dreams to warn her. Odd how the old man she described in her dream looked like the guy who was guarding the ice-cream truck.

"You look very nice tonight. But I know you're in a hurry."

Who was that guy?

It is a mystery that will have to be solved another time.

I make no effort to hide my approach. I know it would be useless to do so. Nevertheless I move as a human moves. My steps are tentative, my breathing tight. The muscles of my face are pinched with anxiety and my shoulders are slumped forward in defeat. Yet my performance goes unheeded as Kalika continues to feed the birds and doesn't glance up until

I am practically on top of them. I pause twenty feet short of the end of the pier. By this time Seymour is looking at me with a mixture of hope and terror. He cannot help but notice I don't have the child with me. The sight of Eric's spurting arteries must have dug deep into his brain. He has little of his usual confidence, although he struggles to make up for it. He forces a smile.

"I'm glad you're not late," he says, and gestures to the moon, which was full the previous night, when Paula's child was born. "Lovely evening, isn't it?"

"I am here," I say to Kalika. "Let him go."

She stares at me now, a handful of pigeons still pecking at the crumbs beside her sandaled feet. Her long white dress—I have never seen it before—is beautiful on her flawless figure, the silky material moving in the moonlit breeze, hugging her mature curves. The birds scatter as she brushes her hands and slowly rises.

"I did not think you would bring the child," she says calmly.

"But I came myself. Release Seymour."

"Why should I?"

"Because I am your mother and I'm requesting this. That should be reason enough."

"It's not."

"He's young. He should not be brought into our affairs."

At that Kalika smiles faintly. "I am young as well, Mother. I should be forgiven any indiscretions I might have committed during my short life."

"Do you need my forgiveness?"

"I suppose not." There is one bird that continues to eat at her feet. Kalika bends back down, plucks it into her hands, and straightens. She strokes the pigeon's feathers and whispers something in its ear. Then she speaks to me. "You should know by now that it's not a good idea to lie to me."

"You force me to lie to you," I say. "Your complaint is absurd."

"Still, it's your habit. You have lied through the ages. You see nothing wrong in it."

"I would have told a million lies to have saved that boy's life." I add, "But you must know I hate to lie to those I love."

Kalika continues to stroke the bird. "Do you love me, Mother?"

"Yes."

She nods in approval. "The truth. Do you love Seymour?"

"Yes."

"Would you be upset if I ripped off his head?"

"I hope this is not a trick question," Seymour mutters.

"You must not hurt him," I say. "He's my friend, and he's done nothing to you. Let him go now and we can talk about the child."

Kalika is once again the master manipulator. She holds up the pigeon. "What about this bird? Should I let it go? Just let it fly away and complete this particular birth? You should know, *Old One*, that it doesn't matter if I do or if I don't. Whenever the bird dies, the bird will simply be reborn. It is the same with humans. If you kill one, it will in time be reincarnated in another body. Perhaps Eric and Billy will both be reborn in better conditions. Eric was not in the best shape when he died." She pauses and coos in the bird's ear again. "What do you think, Mother?"

There is something disturbing in her question, in her examples, besides the obvious. Maybe she is honestly trying to tell me something about her inner state, who she is, what she really is. It is said many times in the Vedas that whenever a demon dies in Krishna's hands, that demon gains instant liberation. But there are fewer books written about Kali's incarnation, her many exploits; and I am not yet ready to accept that my daughter is in fact the real Kali. Of course, I could ask her directly but the mere thought of doing so fills me with apprehension. Many things do: the way she holds the bird close to her mouth; her quick glances at Seymour; the steadiness of her gaze as she studies me, missing nothing. It is impossible to gauge what she will do next, and when she will do it. I try as best I can to answer her, trying to think what Krishna would say to her. Really, I am no saint; I cannot preach morality without sounding like a hypocrite.

"There is a meaning behind each life," I say. "A purpose. It doesn't matter if humans or birds live thousands of lives before they return to God. Each life is valued. Each time you take one, you incur bad karma."

"That is not so." She brushes the bird against the

side of her face. "Karma does not touch me. Karma is for humans, and vampires."

She reproaches me, I realize, for being exactly what I tried not to be. "These last few centuries I have seldom killed without strong reason," I say.

"Eric and Billy died for a reason," she says.

"For what reason did Eric die?"

"To inspire you."

I am disgusted. "Do I look inspired?"

"Yes," she says. "But you did not answer my earlier question, about Seymour's head." She takes a dangerous step toward him. Seymour jumps and I don't blame him. But I catch his eye; I don't want him to make any more sudden moves. Kalika continues, "Would you be upset if I ripped it off?"

I have a choice to make and I must make it quickly. Before she can move any closer to Seymour, I can attack. If I leap forward, I can kick her in the nose and send her nasal cartilage into her brain and kill her. Seymour wouldn't even see my blow. Kalika would simply be dead. But I am still twenty feet from my daughter, not an ideal distance. She could react in time and deflect my blow. Then, before I could recover, Seymour would die.

I decided to wait. To be patient.

I wonder if my patience is grounded in my attachment to Kalika.

She is my daughter. How can I kill her?

"Yes," I say. "You know I would be upset."

Kalika squeezes the pigeon gently. "Would you be upset if I ripped this bird's head off?"

I am annoyed. "Why do you ask these silly questions?"

"To hear your answers."

"This sounds like a trick question," Seymour warns.

I hesitate. He's right. "If there is no reason to kill it, I would say you should leave it alone."

"Answer my question," she says.

"I would not be upset if you killed the bird."

Kalika rips the bird's head off. The tearing bone and tissue make a faint nauseating sound. Blood splashes over the front of my daughter's pretty white dress. Seymour almost faints. Casually, while still watching me, Kalika throws the remains of the bird over her shoulder and into the dark water below. It is only then I catch a glimmer of red light deep inside her pupils. The fire at the end of time, the Vedas call it. The smoky shadow of the final twilight. Kalika knows I see it for she smiles at me.

"You look upset, Mother," she says.

"You are cruel," I say. "Cruelness without rational thought is not far from insanity."

"I told you, I have my reasons." She wipes the blood on the left side of her face. "Tell me where Paula Ramirez's child is."

I glance at Seymour. "I can't," I say.

"Damn," he whispers, and he's not being funny.

"Why do you assume I am going to harm this child?" she asks.

"Because of your previous erratic behavior," I reply.

"If I had not killed Billy, you would not be here tonight. If I had not killed Eric, you would also not be here tonight."

"I didn't need Eric's death to survive the last twenty-four hours."

Kalika teases without inflection. "Really?"

She may be hinting at the fact that I am now a vampire, that I would never have gone through with the transformation without the motivation Eric's horrible murder gave me. She would be right on that point, if it is what she is hinting at. But I continue to hope she thinks I'm helpless. I feel I must attack soon, favorable position or not. The bird's death has not increased my faith in her nonviolent nature. She waits for me to respond.

"I cannot trust you around Paula's baby," I say, taking a step closer. "Surely you must understand that." When she doesn't answer right away, I ask, "What did you do to the police?"

"I fulfilled their karma."

"That's no answer."

Kalika moves closer to Seymour, standing now five feet from his left side. He can't even look at her. Only at me, the creature who saved him from AIDS, who inspires his stories, his savior and his muse. His eyes beg me for a miracle.

"What if I promise you that I will not hurt the child," Kalika says. "Will you take me to him?"

"No. I can't."

She acts mildly surprised. But there is no real emotion in her voice or on her face. Human expressions are merely tools to her. I doubt she feels anything at all, while eating or reading, walking or killing.

"No?" Kalika says. "Have I ever lied to you before?" She moves her arms as if stretching them. Blood drips from her sharp fingernails. In a microsecond, I know, she can reach out and grab Seymour and then it will all be over. She adds, "I am your daughter, but I do not have your habit of lying."

"Kalika," I plead. "Be reasonable. You refuse to tell me why you want to see this child. I can only conclude that you intend to harm it." I pause. "Is that not true?"

"Your question is meaningless to me."

I take another step forward. She is now only twelve feet away, but I want to be closer still. "What is so special about this child?" I ask. "You can at least tell me that."

"No."

"Why not?"

She is subtly amused. "It's forbidden."

"Oh, and killing innocent people isn't? Forbidden by whom?"

"You wouldn't understand." She pauses. "Where's Ray?"

I freeze in midstep. "He's gone."

She seems to understand. "He was forbidden." She glances at Seymour, smiles at him actually as a pretty girl might while flirting. But the words that come out of her mouth next are far from nice. They sound like a warning. She says, "Certain things, once broken, are better left unfixed."

The decision is made for me. Something in her tone tells me she is going to reach for Seymour and that his head will go over the railing as the bird's did—and with the same emotional impact on Kalika. I attack.

My reclaimed vampiric body is no stranger to me. I have not needed time to readapt to it. Indeed it feels almost more natural than it used to. But I definitely decide to stick with an old technique of killing—the nose into the brain thrust. It is straightforward and effective. My only trouble—as I tense my muscles to respond—is that I still love her.

Kalika begins to reach out with her right arm.

I leap up and forward. My lift off the ground is effortless. If I were taped and the video later slowed down for viewing, the human eye would assume that gravity had no effect on me. Of course this is not true—I cannot fly. Only strength is responsible for the illusion. I whip toward Kalika, my right foot the hammer of Thor. I cock it back—it will soon be over.

But somewhere in the air I hesitate. Just slightly.

Probably it makes no difference, but I will never know.

The red flames smolder deep in Kalika's eyes.

My divine hammer is forged of crude iron ore. My daughter grabs my foot before it can reach her face. Real time returns, and I begin a slow horizontal fall, helpless as she grips my foot tighter. Seymour cries in horror and my own cry is one of excruciating pain. She has twisted my ankle almost to the breaking point. I hit the asphalt with the flat of my back and the back of my skull. Kalika towers over me, still holding onto my boot. Her expression is surprisingly gentle.

"Does it hurt?" she asks.

I grimace. "Yes."

Kalika breaks my ankle. I hear the bones snap like kindling wood in a fire, and a wave of red agony slams up my leg and into my brain. As I writhe on the ground, she takes a step back and patiently watches me, never far from Seymour's side. She knows vampires. The pain is intense but it doesn't take long before I begin to heal. The effect of Yaksha's blood on my system no doubt speeds up the process. In two minutes I am able to stand and put weight on the ankle. But I will not be kicking her again in the next few minutes, and she knows it.

Kalika grabs Seymour by the left arm.

His mouth goes wide in shock.

"I will not ask you again what I want to know," she says.

I try to stand straight. Insolence enters my tone. "You know what bugs me most about you? You always hide behind a human shield. I'm here and you're there. Why don't we just settle this between us? That is, if you've got the guts, girl."

Kalika seems to approve of my challenge. She smiles and this particular smile seems genuine. But I'm not sure if it is good to push her into too happy a mood for she suddenly reaches over, picks Seymour up with one hand by grabbing his shirt, and throws him over the side of the pier. The move is so unexpected that I stand stunned for a second. I hurry to the railing in time to see Seymour strike the water. She threw him hard and high—he takes a long time to return to the surface. He coughs as he does so and flays about in the dark but he seems to be all right. I hope he is not like Joel who couldn't swim.

"Seymour!" I call.

He responds with something unintelligible, but sounds OK.

Kalika stands beside me. "He has a sense of humor," she says.

"Thank you for sparing him." The pier is long and the water is cold. I hope he is able to make it to shore. I add, "Thanks for giving him a chance."

"Gratitude means nothing to me," she says.

I am curious. "What does have meaning to you?"

"The essence of all things. The essence does not judge. It is not impressed by actions, nor does it reward inaction." She shrugs. "It just is, as I am."

"I can't tell you where the baby is. I deliberately told Paula not to tell me where she was going. They could be in Canada by now or in Mexico."

Kalika is not disturbed by my revelations. "I know there is something you are not telling me. It relates to future contact with the child. You told Paula one other thing besides what you just said. What was it?"

"There was nothing else."

"You are lying," she says.

"So I lie? What are you going to about it? I'm not going to tell you anything. And if you kill me you still won't get the information you want." I pause. "But I can't believe that even you would kill your own mother."

She reaches out and touches my long blond hair with her bloody hand. "You are beautiful, Sita. You have lived through an entire age. You have outsmarted men and women of all nationalities, in all countries and times. You even tricked your creator into releasing you from his vow to Krishna."

"I did not trick Yaksha. I saved him."

She continues to play with my hair. "As you say, Mother. You have faith in what you know and what you remember. But my memory is older, far older, and death or the threat of death is not the only means of persuasion I have at my disposal." She tugs lightly on my hair. "You must know by now that I am not simply a vampire."

"What are you then?"

She takes my chin in her hand. "Look into my eyes and you will see."

"No. Wait!"

"Look, Mother." She twists my head around and catches my eyes. There is no question of my looking away. It is not an option. The blue-black of her eyes have the pull of a black hole, the grip of the primordial seed that gave birth to the universe. The power that emanates from them is cosmic. They shine with colors the spectrum has forgotten. Yet they are such beautiful eyes, really, those of an innocent girl, and I fall in love with them all over again. From far away I hear my daughter's voice, and it is the voice of thunder echoing and also the mere whisper of a baby falling asleep in my lap in the middle of the night. "Behold your child," she says.

I look; I must look.

There are planets, stars, galaxies, and they are seemingly endless. Yet beyond them all, beyond the backbone of the sky, as the Vedas say, is the funeral pyre. There sits Mother Kali with her Lord Kala, who destroys time itself. As each of the planets slowly dies and each sun gradually expands into a red dwarf, the flames that signal the end of creation begin to burn. They lick the frozen asteroids and melt the lost comets. And there in that absolute space Kali collects the ash of the dead creation and the skulls of forgotten souls. She saves them for another time, when the worlds will breathe again, and people will once again look up at the sky and wonder what lies beyond the stars. But none of these people will know that it was Kali who remembered them when they were ash. None of them will know who buried them when there was no one left to cover their graves. Even if they did remember, none of them would worship the great Kali because they would be too afraid of her.

I feel afraid as I remember her.

As she asks me to remember.

There is another voice in the sky.

I think it is my own. The shock breaks the vision.

I stumble back from my daughter. "You are Kali!" I gasp.

She just looks at me. "You have told me the phone number Paula will call in one month." She turns away. "That's all I wanted to know."

It is hard to throw off the power of the vision.

"Wait. Please? Kalika!"

She glances over her shoulder. "Yes, Mother?"

"Who was the child?"

"Do you really need to know?"

"Yes."

"The knowledge will cost you."

"I need to know!" I cry.

In response Kalika steps to the end of the pier. There she kneels and pulls a board free. It is an old board, long and narrow, but as she works it in her powerful fingers it begins to resemble something I know all too well from more superstitious eras. Too late I realize she has fashioned a stake. She raises the tiny spear over her head and lets fly with it.

The stake goes into the water.

Into Seymour's back. He cries out and sinks.

"No!" I scream.

Kalika stares at me a moment. "I told you it would cost you." She turns away. "I don't lie, Mother."

My ankle is not fully recovered but I am still a strong vampire. Leaping over the side of the pier, I hit the cold salt water not far from where Seymour flounders two feet below the surface. Pulling him up for air, I hear him gasp in pain. My eyes see as well in the dark as in the daylight. The stake has pierced his lower spine. The tip protrudes from where his belly button should be. His blood flows like water from a broken faucet.

"This hurts," he says.

"Seymour," I cry as I struggle to keep him afloat, "you have to stay with me. If I can get you to shore, I can save you."

He reaches for the stake and moans in pain. "Pull it out."

"No. You'll bleed to death in seconds. I can take it out only when we reach the beach. You must hold on to me so that I can swim as fast as possible. Listen to me, Seymour!"

But he is already going into shock. "Help me, Sita," he chokes.

"No!" I slap him. "Stay with me. I'll get you to shore." Then, wrapping my right arm around him, I begin to swim as fast as I can with one free arm and two boot-clad feet. But speed in the water is not Seymour's friend. As I kick toward the beach, the pressure of the passing water on the stake makes him swoon in agony. The rushing water also increases his loss of blood. Yet I feel I have no choice but to hurry.

"Stop, Sita," he gasps as he starts to faint. "I can't stand it."

"You can stand it. This time you're the hero in my story. You can write it all down later. This pain will not last and you will laugh about it in a few days. Because tonight you're going to get what you've always wanted. You're going to become a vampire."

He is interested, although he is clearly dying. The beach is still two hundred yards away. "Really?" he mumbles. "A real vampire?"

"Yes! You'll be able to stay out all night and party and you won't ever get old and ugly. We'll travel the world and we'll have more fun than you can imagine. Seymour?"

"Party," he says faintly, his face sagging into the water. Having to hold his mouth up slows me down even more but I keep kicking. I imagine an observer on the pier would think a power boat were about to ram the beach. The sand is only a hundred yards away now.

"Hang in there," I tell him.

Finally, when we are in five feet of water, I am able

to put my feet down. I carry him to the beach and carefully lay him on his right side. There is no one around to help us. His blood continues to gush out around the edges of the wooden stake, at the front as well as at the back. He is the color of refined flour. He hardly breathes, and though I yell in his ear I have to wonder if he is not already beyond hearing. Already beyond even the power of my blood. The situation is worse than it was with Ray and Joel. Neither of them had an object implanted in them. Even vampire flesh cannot heal around such an object, and yet I fear I cannot simply pull it out. I feel his life will spill out with it and be lost on the cold sand.

"Seymour!" I cry. "Come back to me!"

A minute later, when all seems lost, when he isn't even breathing, my prayer is mysteriously answered. He opens his eyes and looks up at me. He even grins his old Seymour grin, which usually makes me want to laugh and hit him at the same time. Yet this time I choke back the tears. The chill on his flesh, I know, is from the touch of the Grim Reaper. Death stands between us and it will not step aside even for a vampire.

"Seymour," I say, "how are you?"

"Fine. The pain has stopped."

"Good."

"But I feel cold." A tremor shakes his body. Dark blood spills over his lips. "Is this normal?"

"Yes. It is perfectly normal." He does not feel the stake now, or even recognize how grave his condition is. He thinks I gave him my blood while he was unconscious. He tries to squeeze my hand but he is too weak. Somehow he manages to keep talking.

"Will I live forever now?" he asks.

"Yes." I bury my face in his. "Forever and ever."

His eyes close. "I will love you that long, Sita."

"Me, too," I whisper. "Me, too."

We speak no more, Seymour and I.

He dies a minute later, in my arms.

Epilogue ⟞

His body I take to a place high in the mountains where I often walked when I lived in Los Angeles. On a bluff, with a view of the desert on one side and the city on the other, I build a funeral pyre from wood I am able to gather in the immediate area. Seymour rests comfortably on top of my construction. At the beach I had removed the bloody stake and thrown it away. He is able to lie on his back and I fold his hands over his big heart.

"You," I say. "You were the best."

There is a wooden match in my right hand, but somehow I am unable to light it. His face looks so peaceful I can't stop staring at him. But I realize the day is moving on, and that the wind will soon pick up. The flames should finish their work before then. Seymour always loved the woods, and wouldn't have wanted them harmed by a raging forest fire. He loved so many things, and I was happy to be one of them.

I strike the match on the bark of a tree.

It burns bright red, and I can't help but think of Kali.

Many things pass through my mind right then.

Many question and so few answers.

Yet I let the flame burn down to my fingertips.

There is pain, a little smoke. The match dies.

And from my pocket I withdraw the vial of blood.

Number seven. *Ramirez*. I look up.

"What is the cost, Kalika?" I ask the sky.

After opening the vial, I pour half the blood over Seymour's wound, and the other half down his throat. Then I close my eyes and walk away and stand silently behind a tall tree for five minutes. Some mysteries are best left unexplained. My hope refuses to be crushed. I have found love and lost love, but perhaps what I have finally rediscovered is my faith in love. I stand and pray—not for bliss or miracles—I simply pray and that is enough.

Finally I walk back to the funeral pyre.

Seymour is sitting up on the wood and looking at me. His fatal wound has healed.

"How did we get here?" he asks.
Of course I have to laugh. "It's a long story," I say.
But I wonder how to finish the story for him.
I still wonder who the child is.
More, I wonder who he *was*.

———————

Look for Christopher Pike's

The Last Vampire 5
EVIL THIRST

Coming mid-June 1996

and

The Last Vampire 6
CREATURES OF FOREVER

Coming mid-August 1996

———————

About the Author

CHRISTOPHER PIKE was born in Brooklyn, New York, but grew up in Los Angeles, where he lives to this day. Prior to becoming a writer, he worked in a factory, painted houses, and programmed computers. His hobbies include astronomy, meditating, running, playing with his nieces and nephews, and making sure his books are prominently displayed in local bookstores. He is the author of *Last Act, Spellbound, Gimme a Kiss, Remember Me, Scavenger Hunt, Final Friends* 1, 2, and 3, *Fall into Darkness, See You Later, Witch, Die Softly, Bury Me Deep, Whisper of Death, Chain Letter 2: The Ancient Evil, Master of Murder, Monster, Road to Nowhere, The Eternal Enemy, The Immortal, The Wicked Heart, The Midnight Club, The Last Vampire, The Last Vampire 2: Black Blood, The Last Vampire 3: Red Dice, Remember Me 2: The Return, Remember Me 3: The Last Story, The Lost Mind, The Visitor* and *The Last Vampire 4: Phantom*, all available from Archway Paperbacks. *Slumber Party, Weekend, Chain Letter*, and *Sati*—an adult novel about a very unusual lady—are also by Mr. Pike.

Christopher Pike presents....
a frighteningly fun new series for your younger brothers and sisters!

SPOOKSVILLE™

1 The Secret Path
53725-3/$3.50

2 The Howling Ghost
53726-1/$3.50

3 The Haunted Cave
53727-X/$3.50

4 Aliens in the Sky
53728-8/$3.99

5 The Cold People
55064-0/$3.99

6 The Witch's Revenge
55065-9/$3.99

7 Fright Night
52947-1/$3.99

8 The Little People
55067-5/$3.99

A MINSTREL® BOOK
Published by Pocket Books

Step into my nightmares. . . .

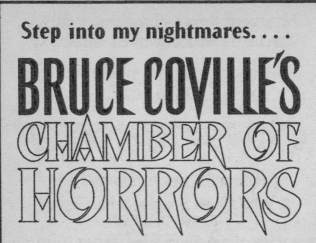

BRUCE COVILLE'S CHAMBER OF HORRORS

- ❑ **#1 Amulet of Doom**
  53637-0/$3.99
- ❑ **#2 Spirits and Spells**
  53638-9/$3.99

and look for

#3 Eyes of the Tarot
Coming mid-May 1996

From Archway Paperbacks
Published by Pocket Books